The Portrait

By Danielle Steel

THE PORTRAIT • FOR RICHER FOR POORER • A MOTHER'S LOVE
A MIND OF HER OWN • FAR FROM HOME • NEVER SAY NEVER • TRIAL BY FIRE
TRIANGLE • JOY • RESURRECTION • ONLY THE BRAVE • NEVER TOO LATE
UPSIDE DOWN • THE BALL AT VERSAILLES • SECOND ACT • HAPPINESS • PALAZZO
THE WEDDING PLANNER • WORTHY OPPONENTS • WITHOUT A TRACE
THE WHITTIERS • THE HIGH NOTES • THE CHALLENGE • SUSPECTS • BEAUTIFUL
HIGH STAKES • INVISIBLE • FLYING ANGELS • THE BUTLER • COMPLICATIONS
NINE LIVES • FINDING ASHLEY • THE AFFAIR • NEIGHBORS • ALL THAT GLITTERS
ROYAL • DADDY'S GIRLS • THE WEDDING DRESS • THE NUMBERS GAME
MORAL COMPASS • SPY • CHILD'S PLAY • THE DARK SIDE • LOST AND FOUND
BLESSING IN DISGUISE • SILENT NIGHT • TURNING POINT • BEAUCHAMP HALL
IN HIS FATHER'S FOOTSTEPS • THE GOOD FIGHT • THE CAST • ACCIDENTAL HEROES
FALL FROM GRACE • PAST PERFECT • FAIRYTALE • THE RIGHT TIME • THE DUCHESS
AGAINST ALL ODDS • DANGEROUS GAMES • THE MISTRESS • THE AWARD
RUSHING WATERS • MAGIC • THE APARTMENT • PROPERTY OF A NOBLEWOMAN
BLUE • PRECIOUS GIFTS • UNDERCOVER • COUNTRY • PRODIGAL SON • PEGASUS
A PERFECT LIFE • POWER PLAY • WINNERS • FIRST SIGHT • UNTIL THE END OF TIME
THE SINS OF THE MOTHER • FRIENDS FOREVER • BETRAYAL • HOTEL VENDÔME
HAPPY BIRTHDAY • 44 CHARLES STREET • LEGACY • FAMILY TIES • BIG GIRL
SOUTHERN LIGHTS • MATTERS OF THE HEART • ONE DAY AT A TIME
A GOOD WOMAN • ROGUE • HONOR THYSELF • AMAZING GRACE • BUNGALOW 2
SISTERS • H.R.H. • COMING OUT • THE HOUSE • TOXIC BACHELORS • MIRACLE
IMPOSSIBLE • ECHOES • SECOND CHANCE • RANSOM • SAFE HARBOUR
JOHNNY ANGEL • DATING GAME • ANSWERED PRAYERS • SUNSET IN ST. TROPEZ
THE COTTAGE • THE KISS • LEAP OF FAITH • LONE EAGLE • JOURNEY
THE HOUSE ON HOPE STREET • THE WEDDING • IRRESISTIBLE FORCES • GRANNY DAN
BITTERSWEET • MIRROR IMAGE • THE KLONE AND I • THE LONG ROAD HOME
THE GHOST • SPECIAL DELIVERY • THE RANCH • SILENT HONOR • MALICE
FIVE DAYS IN PARIS • LIGHTNING • WINGS • THE GIFT • ACCIDENT • VANISHED
MIXED BLESSINGS • JEWELS • NO GREATER LOVE • HEARTBEAT • MESSAGE FROM NAM
DADDY • STAR • ZOYA • KALEIDOSCOPE • FINE THINGS • WANDERLUST • SECRETS
FAMILY ALBUM • FULL CIRCLE • CHANGES • THURSTON HOUSE • CROSSINGS
ONCE IN A LIFETIME • A PERFECT STRANGER • REMEMBRANCE
PALOMINO • LOVE: *POEMS* • THE RING • LOVING • TO LOVE AGAIN
SUMMER'S END • SEASON OF PASSION • THE PROMISE
NOW AND FOREVER • PASSION'S PROMISE • GOING HOME

Nonfiction

EXPECT A MIRACLE: *Quotations to Live and Love By*
PURE JOY: *The Dogs We Love*
A GIFT OF HOPE: *Helping the Homeless*
HIS BRIGHT LIGHT: *The Story of Nick Traina*

For Children

PRETTY MINNIE IN PARIS • PRETTY MINNIE IN HOLLYWOOD

DANIELLE STEEL

The Portrait

A Novel

Delacorte Press
New York

Delacorte Press
An imprint of Random House
A division of Penguin Random House LLC
1745 Broadway, New York, NY 10019
randomhousebooks.com
penguinrandomhouse.com

Copyright © 2025 by Danielle Steel

Penguin Random House values and supports copyright. Copyright fuels creativity, encourages diverse voices, promotes free speech, and creates a vibrant culture. Thank you for buying an authorized edition of this book and for complying with copyright laws by not reproducing, scanning, or distributing any part of it in any form without permission. You are supporting writers and allowing Penguin Random House to continue to publish books for every reader. Please note that no part of this book may be used or reproduced in any manner for the purpose of training artificial intelligence technologies or systems.

DELACORTE PRESS is a registered trademark and the DP colophon is a trademark of Penguin Random House LLC.

Hardcover ISBN 978-0-593-49876-7
Ebook ISBN 978-0-593-49877-4

Printed in the United States of America on acid-free paper

246897531

First Edition

The authorized representative in the EU for product safety and compliance is Penguin Random House Ireland, Morrison Chambers, 32 Nassau Street, Dublin D02 YH68, Ireland.
https://eu-contact.penguin.ie

To my darling children
Beatie, Trevor, Todd,
Nick, Samantha, Victoria,
Vanessa, Maxx, and Zara,

May you be brave and happy
and well-loved and cherished.

With all my love and heart,
I wish you happy endings
and that all your dreams come true.

Mom / D.S.

Silence

Along the jagged edges
of your silences,
my heart snags,
soars and stumbles,
while trying to back away
and give you space
and let you breathe,
I trip
and sail headlong
into your arms
and see you
so close to me,
I can hear you
breathe,
I can hear
your heart,
next to mine,
sounding like one,
a single beat
like a drum,
wondering if
you will return,
if you will come
close to me again,
or run,
never sure
which way you'll turn,
you hide

in the silences,
the sound
of your heartbeat
in my ears,
your face
in my eyes,
my own heart
in your hands,
to toss away,
dismiss,
forget the reality
of me,
a pebble in your path,
a memory,
am I to become
someone
you once knew,
as I wait silently
in the shadows,
hand outstretched
to you
to love,
to comfort,
to walk the path
with you,
share your pain
and help you find
your way
back into the sunlight
where you will find

your voice again
and bring me back
into the present
where the music
and voices
await us.
     D.S.

The Portrait

Chapter 1

The Grace Cathedral choir in San Francisco was singing "Amazing Grace" as Charles Mackenzie Taylor stood at his father's funeral, letting his thoughts drift to the familiar music. It was a beautiful warm June day. His father, Patrick Taylor, had been a fierce and bold leader, greatly respected in the community, head of Golden State Bank, which his own grandfather had founded, and which three generations of Taylor men had owned and run. It had been one of the largest commercial banks in California since the Gold Rush days. Patrick had died at eighty-five after a year-long bout with cancer. He was a force to be reckoned with and a hard man to please. He had continued to go to the office until his last few months, and the bank was officially run by a highly experienced CEO and a competent staff, overseen by a board of directors, of which Patrick had been chairman.

Charles was Patrick's only child, brilliant in his own right, with no interest whatsoever in the family bank or the world of finance, unlike all his male ancestors before him. He would be the first Taylor heir who would never run the bank, although out of a sense of duty and a recent promise to his father, he had agreed to step into his father's shoes as chairman of the board, which he dreaded. Several members of the board were close to his father's age, had conservative, antiquated ideas, and took rigid positions on most things, and Charles found them as difficult to get along with as his father had been. The rest of the board were CEOs of large companies, leaders of the financial community, and included two women, one of whom was the widow of one of their largest investment clients, and the other of whom ran a hedge fund. They all had the right credentials, very little imagination, if any, and no desire to do anything innovative. Charles felt as though he couldn't breathe whenever he walked into his father's office. They had never gotten along. It was no secret that Patrick had never approved of him, and now Charles had to run the board.

At forty-nine, Charles had been a renegade all his life, with a passion for new ideas and an unfailing instinct for the needs and trends of the future. Despite the trust he had been left by his grandparents and his father, he had made his own fortune doing what he loved, starting new businesses. His education had been almost identical to his father's, but Charlie had done entirely different things with his. He had attended Princeton as an undergraduate, then Harvard Business School in the entrepreneurial program, which Patrick said was unnecessary, with a bank to run. Charlie had started to build his future as a junior at Princeton, when he created a delivery service for fellow students, bringing them everything from food to medicine and pharmaceutical needs,

The Portrait

including industrial quantities of condoms, and eventually branching out to deliver everything from mattresses to office equipment. He expanded his business model through friends at other universities, and eventually had nearly a hundred branches throughout the United States. He sold the business for what even his father considered an astounding amount of money. It was one of the earliest and most successful startups, and set the bar high for others who followed in his footsteps with their own startups. The concept was simple and it worked. During the years he was growing the business, Charlie's father referred to him as The Delivery Boy, and was furious when the business kept Charlie from taking his place at the bank, and gave him an excuse not to. It took his father years to admit to himself that Charlie was never going to be a part of the family business, and that there had never been any hope of it. Charlie was destined to fly in his own skies, on wings broader than his father's.

By the time Charlie got to business school, he was already a very rich man from the sale of his startup, not even considering his trusts. But he wanted the same credentials as his ancestors. He set up another startup, this time in healthier fast food, at first in the United States and eventually worldwide. It wasn't an elegant, distinguished way to make a fortune, but it was extremely efficient. He hadn't sold the company yet, had hung onto it for a long time and refused several offers, but it was ultimately his plan to sell. He would launch another startup afterward. He was thinking about that now and wasn't sure which new direction he would take. He liked shiny new ideas that others hadn't thought of yet. Simple ideas that worked. He had a passion for business. He had put his heart and soul into it. Business was his first love. He loved everything about it.

Being at his father's funeral brought back memories of his mother. She had died when he was thirteen. His memories of her had faded now, but he remembered her as a beautiful, lovely, gentle, kind, loving woman, everything his father wasn't. His father was cold and austere, unbending and unforgiving. He had never remarried. Three months after Charlie's mother died, his father had sent him to St. Paul's, a boarding school in the East and another family tradition. It was a long way from San Francisco, and no one ever visited him there. Charlie felt his mother's absence acutely that first year. Time had helped heal the wound, but he had never really gone home again, except for short visits. After St. Paul's, he had gone to Princeton, where he had stayed for an extra year to run his fledgling delivery business, and then gone on to Harvard Business School. His father had a large, handsome house in San Francisco, where Charlie had lived before he left for school and stayed during his visits, but after business school, Charlie had bought a very beautiful home in Atherton and set up offices in Palo Alto in Silicon Valley, home to venture capital and many startups.

He had married young, on an impulse at twenty-six, when he was finishing business school for his MBA. He'd been dating Faye, a girl five years older than he was, from a family of bankers in New York. Her family was similar to his, though slightly less austere. She was an only child like him, and she was in the throes of a wildly rebellious stage. Once at Harvard, she dyed her hair purple, and they had fun together. She was smart, an outstanding law student, and wanted to save the world. They'd only been dating

The Portrait

for a few months at school, on a boring holiday weekend, when Charlie convinced her to fly to Las Vegas with him. It sounded like a great idea. They got outrageously drunk, wound up at the Elvis Chapel, which they thought was hysterically funny, and woke up married. Predictably, neither family was pleased, and called them irresponsible. Both sets of parents wanted them to have the marriage annulled, but both families were respectable. Faye was incredibly smart and graduated from Harvard Law School at the top of her class, and she and Charlie decided to give the marriage a try. It worked for a while, but not for long. Her rebelliousness faded when they moved to California and she got a job at one of the most important venture capital firms in Silicon Valley. Charlie had convinced her to come west and look for a job in tech when he went back to San Francisco. She turned into her parents almost immediately, with conservative views. Her purple hair disappeared, along with almost everything else he had liked about her. She thought fast food was beneath him, although it was earning him millions. She turned out to be critical and cold, instead of fun and sexy as she had been at Harvard. They were both considering divorce by the end of the first year, and regretting their rash leap into marriage, when Faye discovered she was pregnant, and they decided to stick with it.

Neither of them was thrilled at the prospect of the pregnancy, and a child, but they both fell in love with baby Liam. Faye went back to work immediately. The baby had arrived three weeks early when she was on a road tour for an IPO, to take a company public, and he had to stay in the hospital for a month. Charlie and Faye made a schedule to take turns visiting him daily, but their work schedules were ferocious, and Charlie traveled all the time. He discovered then that he had more parental instincts than Faye, who appeared to have none. She was more interested in her job and career than a baby, and Charlie had little time to devote to him.

The child was entirely cared for by a series of nannies. Liam was a bright boy and an undemanding child, who learned early on to be self-sufficient. He expected little of his parents. Faye insisted on sending him east to boarding school at Andover, where her father had gone. When Liam left at fourteen, Charlie missed him, but he knew from his own experience that it was already too late. They had missed the boat, and like both his parents, Liam was an only child. Charlie knew when Liam left that he would never be home again for long. The years had flown by. Liam had just graduated from Yale, was going back to Yale for graduate school to study architecture, and was leaving for Europe in a few days with friends to visit châteaux in France and castles in England, as a prelude to his graduate studies. Amazingly, Liam was good-natured, forgiving, and independent, and never seemed to hold Charlie and Faye's neglectful parenting against them. He wasn't close to them, but he didn't resent them either. He was mature and philosophical about their failings and accepted them as they were.

Charlie was a strikingly handsome man with a full head of dark hair, tall, with a well-toned athletic body, and electric blue eyes. Faye was a very fair blonde with skin that hadn't aged well, and she paid little attention to her looks. She was fifty-four now, and looked slightly older. She had spent a lifetime working among men, and had played down her feminine side to compete with them. Liam looked like his father, with his mother's blond hair and his father's blue eyes.

Both Charlie and Faye dove into their careers with a vengeance as soon as they left grad school. It left them little time to spend with each other, and once Liam was born they seemed to drift even further apart. Charlie was aware of it, but did nothing about it. Faye seemed not to notice, or mind. She'd become a partner of the firm very early, and all her energies were spent there.

For a moment, when Liam left for boarding school after fifteen years of marriage, they thought that their relationship might have a renaissance, and they might recapture a warmer time long ago. Instead their lives seemed to get busier than ever, and without Liam's presence as the prime reason for their staying married, they found that they had drifted too far apart and there was nothing left. Their marriage was dead. It was a turning point for both of them. They discussed it one night over dinner in their kitchen. They rarely had time for dinner together and hadn't had dinner as a family in years. The housekeeper cooked for Liam. Faye was out most nights with clients, and Charlie was either out working late, or in another city acquiring another company to add more restaurants. He had built an empire which he ran himself.

Their decision, after several glasses of wine, was to stay together and continue as they were. Faye pointed out that divorce would be costly, inconvenient, time-consuming to work out the finances, and maybe even embarrassing. They stayed together, but once they made the decision for practical reasons, there was no pretense of it being anything more than that. Charlie was never sure if he had ever loved her, and Faye had long since concluded that she didn't love him. Even Liam understood by the time he was in his teens that his parents had a loveless marriage, and there was little in it for him. He loved spending time with his friends' families rather than his own. Other mothers who observed the Taylors with a keen eye saw that they had everything but love. They felt sorry for Liam, but he did well anyway, like a flower growing between rocks, and got what he needed to survive, wherever he could. He was astonishingly self-sufficient for a boy his age, and mature. He had grown up among adults, and he was as bright as his parents.

Charlie and Faye told themselves that they stayed together "for Liam's sake," without the pretense of being close. Their lives were on separate paths, with the occasional social appearance, usually for Charlie's business or hers. Liam wasn't close to either of them. When he wanted advice, he went to teachers or his friends or their parents, not his own. They didn't have time. They were responsible parents—they fed and housed him and paid for his education and holidays, and gave him nothing more. Charlie felt guilty about it sometimes, but Faye never mentioned it. They were three strangers living under the same roof who barely knew each other, each pursuing their own life, and the thread which bound them to each other was very thin.

Charlie had sought amusement and distraction from a wide variety of women over the years, without getting close to them. Something always stopped him, possibly the fact that he was married, although that never discouraged him from dating. Being married relieved him of making any other commitments, which suited him. He made no promises he couldn't keep and didn't wish to. He wanted no complications in his life, nor did he want to mislead anyone. He didn't want or need more than he had. He had never been faithful to Faye, but he respected her as a good friend, even if he didn't love her, and probably never had.

He conducted most of his affairs in other cities, to avoid complications, rather than in San Francisco, where he spent the least amount of time. The affairs lasted a while, and he didn't try to prolong them. He was careful to pick women who didn't expect more of him than he was willing to give. Now and then, he made a mistake, but not often. When he did, and spent time with a woman who had big expectations of him, or was needy, he ended it quickly. He was an expert at ending his affairs smoothly. All of his passion went into his business. The rest was entertainment, or a distraction.

Faye was equally discreet, and neither of them asked the questions they didn't want answers to. Their marriage was a choice, and suited them both. Faye liked the status and comforts it afforded her, regardless of the man. Charlie was a decent person and she admired him enough to stay married to him, no matter what he did on his own. They were a habit neither of them enjoyed or wanted to break.

Charles stood at his father's funeral, looking heartbreakingly handsome, thinking of the practical aspects of his father's death, the things he had to do now.

There were two houses his father owned that he had to sell, and art and objects to send to auction or put in storage for Liam later. Faye didn't like the house in Tahoe and neither did he, or he would have kept it. Once fashionable among the rich, Lake Tahoe was full of tourists now, and people in the camping grounds. And the traffic to get there was terrible. It was overcrowded and overrun.

The strength of Charlie's career had been to think outside the box, solidified by the skills he had learned at Harvard, with his own unfailing instincts and magic added. His work life had all the passion and excitement that his personal life didn't. He loved his work, and his companies were his children and mistresses, the recipients of all the emotions he had never shared with another person. Because of the absence of his mother since the age of thirteen, and his cold father, Charlie had never been shown how to love another human. It was the one instinct he didn't have and what he feared. He preferred to give his heart to what he could control.

His father's death wasn't painful for him, except for the duties he would have to undertake and didn't want, like being chairman of the board. He thought Faye would have done it better. She was more traditional and a better team player, but it was his responsibility, not hers.

Patrick had been an austere, severe, often harsh critic of his son. The two men had never understood each other, nor tried to. Charlie had early on taken pleasure in being a maverick in business—he was good at it and it had served him well.

After the service at Grace Cathedral, which ended with Beethoven's "Ode to Joy," Charlie greeted as many of the seven

The Portrait

hundred people who attended as he could on the way out. His striking good looks made him stand out in the crowd. He was wearing a perfectly tailored black suit made by his tailor in New York, where he kept a Fifth Avenue apartment he used when he did business there. He still traveled most of the time, checking on his offices around the country and the world. He was forty-nine and looked years younger.

At fifty-four, Faye did nothing to hide her age. She dressed in conservative business style. She had sacrificed the frills of femininity in order to let the men she worked with know that she was one of them, and as powerful as any of them. She exuded an aura of strength, intelligence, and seriousness. She wore her blond hair short, used very little makeup, and seemed timeless, not of any particular era. She had worn a plain black suit to the funeral, by no particular designer. She had no interest in fashion. She had more important things to do. She had gotten on well with her father-in-law, better than Charles ever had. Her own parents had died years before, so Liam had just lost the only grandparent he had. Patrick had liked him better than his own son. Patrick had had a hard time warming up to anyone, even his own flesh and blood. It went against the grain.

Charlie, Faye, and Liam left for the cemetery as quickly as they could. The hearse had just pulled away as they came down the steps of the church. The pallbearers had been the men on the board. With Patrick's secretary, Faye had organized a reception for several hundred guests at his home in San Francisco. Charlie was dreading it. It would be stifling, with the rooms full of all the social and banking people that he didn't care about. He had carved out a niche for himself in a very different world of modern, unorthodox, high-tech thinkers, people who had come up from nothing and made incredible fortunes with innovative ideas, not by following in their predecessors' footsteps. They were all the people Patrick disapproved of and didn't understand, like his son.

In time, Charlie intended to step down from the board quietly, but he couldn't do it yet. He had to go through the motions for a year or so. He was going to his father's office the next day, to tie up some loose ends, and then flying to New York that night for meetings. His company was opening twenty more healthy fast-food restaurants in the suburbs of New York, and in the days following, he had meetings planned in Boston, Atlanta, Miami, and Chicago. He had a busy few weeks ahead. Liam was leaving for his trip to Europe to celebrate his recent graduation from Yale. Faye had a new fund she was opening to her firm's investors. They each had their own plans and Liam, who was now twenty-two, would be starting his architectural studies back at Yale in the fall, building his future.

As Charlie left the church, a boyhood friend, Adam Stein, stopped him briefly with a smile. They still saw each other for lunch from time to time. He was the managing partner of the biggest law firm in the city, and Charlie's lawyer.

"I'm sorry, Charlie," he said respectfully, although he knew that Charlie was less so and his father's death was a relief, a release from a relationship that had been painful all his life. "You're up, Mr. Chairman," he said in an undertone, with a teasing glance, and Charlie winced. "I'll call you for a loan next week. Maggie wants me to build a new house in Belvedere. I'm counting on you."

The Portrait

Charlie knew Adam wasn't serious about the loan. He was one of the most successful attorneys in the city.

"I can't wait to turn you down," Charlie quipped back. "And I'm not 'up.'" He and Adam used to play baseball together on their school team. "I'll be out as fast as I can get away with it. I'll be on the road for the next few weeks. They'll do fine without me."

"You'll have to play ball with them at least for a while," Adam reminded him, and Charlie looked pained. Board meetings bored him intensely and never moved fast enough for him, which Adam knew. Charlie thought fast, moved fast, acted decisively. The bank moved with the speed of an iceberg and the members deliberated at length before making any significant decisions, and they were never exciting ones. Acting as chairman, even for a year, was his father's final punishment for him, after a lifetime of them. Charlie had never won his father's approval.

"See you at the house later," Adam said, and patted his friend's arm, as Charlie nodded and moved through the crowd to find Faye and Liam. They were waiting at the car that would take them to the cemetery for the private burial, where it would all finally end, with a handful of earth thrown into the grave, after the minister's last words.

Faye looked at him questioningly, to see if he was okay. Charlie looked as calm and in control as he always was. He had waited forty-nine years for this day, and it had finally come.

They drove to the cemetery without a word, each of them lost in their own thoughts, with nothing they wanted to say to each other. Charlie remembered hazy moments of his mother's funeral and felt a rush of sadness. Faye remembered her own parents, and Liam thought of the grandfather who had always scared him a little but had been kind to him. He would miss him, or miss just knowing he was there.

The silence was familiar to all three of them, and was easier than sharing what they felt—or admitting what they didn't feel, in Charlie's case. The silence was where they each felt safe. After a lifetime of distance between them, they knew there was nothing to say.

Devon Darcy woke up as she did every morning, with daylight streaming into the room, sometimes bright sunshine, and the light from the lamp she left on at night near her bed. She liked knowing where she was immediately on waking. In the darkness, she was haunted by ghosts of the past. She had learned to live with them. There was a tree outside her window that she could see from her bed, and hear the birds perching on it. They started chirping even before daylight.

She lived on the top two floors of a well-kept once-elegant townhouse in the West Village in downtown New York, on the West Side near the Hudson River. It stood in a row of houses like it, and down the street there were shops and restaurants and people. The street was quiet, and the neighborhood alive with old people, mothers and children, runners, dog walkers, and people laughing and talking to each other. She liked that. They were there if she wanted to see them when she took a break from work and went for a walk.

The Portrait

Her cozy bedroom was on the top floor, and on the floor below, she had a large living room with a marble fireplace she never used, tall French windows with beautiful antique satin curtains with tassels, and a dining room she had turned into her studio, filled with blank canvases in a corner, others leaning against the wall, her brushes and paints spread out on a work table, a large comfortable chair for her subjects, her easel, and a number of small portraits hanging on the walls. She was a portrait artist. The canvas she was currently working on was on her easel, with layers of paint on it. She had only just begun to work on the underlayer, and sketched the shapes that would emerge as the subject came to life in her head and on the canvas. When her subjects lived in New York, she met with them once a week for several months, sometimes less if she had a strong connection with them. Those who lived far away spent a morning or afternoon in her studio with her, and she took videos and photographs of them making normal movements and expressions while they talked to her, and she would refer to the photographs later while she painted. They came to life on the canvas.

Between commissions, she painted people she didn't know from drawings she sketched randomly from memory, or as she watched them in restaurants, or parks. She had drawn people since she was a child. It was a gift. She had dreamed of being a ballerina as a little girl, and had painted dancers in every position, like Degas. Now she painted important people, and only accepted the commissions she wanted to, through a highly reputable gallery uptown. She did portraits mostly of men, occasionally of women. She saw into their souls and listened to them during sittings.

Though she'd been a shy child, she had painted the world she observed with startling maturity and insight, which had deepened over the years.

Destiny had dealt Devon a hard hand. Her parents had died in a fire when she was five. She barely remembered them. They lived in New York in a small walk-up apartment in a poor unkempt neighborhood and were both teachers. The building was rundown and caught fire. Devon was saved by the firefighters right before the roof caved in, but they couldn't get to her parents. She still remembered them screaming as the firefighters rushed her away. Her mother was French and her father American. He had no living family. She was sent to Paris to live with her maternal grandmother, who had been a ballet teacher, became a seamstress, and made gowns for society ladies who came to the apartment for fittings. Devon would sketch them while they weren't watching. She loved the way they looked and what they wore, the way they did their hair, and the gowns her grandmother made them.

Her grandmother was strict but kind, and she had recognized Devon's talent. She died when Devon was sixteen. She left enough money for Devon to attend the École des Beaux-Arts, the famous art school, where she was classically trained and learned to master her gift. She married a fellow art student, a sculptor, when she was twenty-two and he was two years older. They had a son, Axel, a year later. Jean-Louis, her husband, was an orphan as she was. He worked as a waiter in a bistro to pay for school, and gave up the Beaux-Arts to support the family when Axel was born. Devon continued her studies and Jean-Louis took care of the baby in the daytime before he went to work at night at the restaurant. He

The Portrait

never complained about the sacrifices he made for them. They managed to pay for food and the rented room they lived in. They had no living relatives, only each other and their son. She barely remembered her parents now, but she remembered Jean-Louis and their son vividly. They lived on in memory, and in her heart.

Jean-Louis was struck by a bus while riding his bike to work on a rainy night when Axel was three. Devon was a widow at twenty-six. She taught drawing at a school to support herself and Axel after Jean-Louis died, and managed to eke out a meager living. She sold drawings at street fairs, quick portraits people liked. Two years after Jean-Louis died, Axel caught meningitis and was gone in twelve hours. At twenty-eight, Devon was alone in the world. It had been fourteen years since then. Axel would have been nineteen now, which was too painful to think of, and she didn't try. It took her a year to get back on her feet and be able to function again. She had made constant sketches of Axel during that year, in order to keep him near her. She didn't want to forget his angelic face with all its expressions. The year was a blur. Now she couldn't make a decent living in France, couldn't bear the memories, and being there without Jean-Louis and Axel. Every park and street was filled with the memories of Axel. She moved to New York, with the little money she had, found the gallery which still represented her now, and when they saw what she was capable of, they began giving her gallery shows. She was forty-two years old now, and had been back in New York for fourteen years.

She had finally reached the pinnacle of success, and now could do only the commissions she wanted and refuse the rest. She researched her subjects carefully, and did those she respected. The results were extraordinary. She didn't paint people she didn't like, because it showed in the work. She saw into their souls, which was part of her gift. She did magnificent paintings that represented her subjects inside and out. They were alive on the canvas and looked as though they would speak at any moment. Her subjects were thrilled with their portraits.

Devon could have done three times as many commissions if she wanted to. She did eight or ten a year, and wanted to be proud of them. The sittings were intense and lengthy, some faster than others. Her years of training, her losses, and years of suffering deepened her skill and mastery of her art. She painted important men and women at the height of their success, people whom she respected for valid reasons, and that were meaningful to her.

She had painted socialites and important commercial, industrial, political, or artistic figures. She had painted a president, and declined another. She had been respected and well known herself for the past seven of the fourteen years in New York. She channeled her subjects' inner being with depth and a highly trained eye. She was never pompous or pretentious, but she was very definite about whom she would paint and whom she wouldn't, and never changed her mind.

She didn't dwell on the past or on her losses, but they were part of her now, and colored how she viewed the world. She wanted to do meaningful work and didn't want to waste time or paint people she didn't admire. She shied away from any real-life involvement with her subjects. Their connection was brief, ephemeral, and existed only on the canvas. They invited her to parties, dinners, weekends, and holidays at their homes but she never went. She lived in her own world. She was no longer a wife or mother, and identified herself only as an artist. She knew the scars she bore intimately, and didn't hide from them, and she was a purist about her work, and the techniques she had learned. She was the harshest critic of her work.

Devon was a beautiful woman with red hair and green eyes the color of Imperial jade. She had delicate fine features, and was lithe and graceful. Her grandmother had paid for ballet lessons for her, from her earnings.

Devon spoke very little to her subjects, but listened to everything they said and translated it into her art.

She ran lightly down the stairs to the kitchen to make herself a strong cup of coffee, and then sat in her nightgown, thinking about the portrait she was about to start. Her subject was a giant of industry who had become an important political figure. He was a powerful man, but seemed like a person of integrity to her. She made no apologies for her work or her boundaries and respected them.

She was having a show at the gallery in two days, and had to prepare for it. She had a lot to do. She had included a series of portraits of children she had done in her spare time. They were beautiful and touching. She knew none of them. They were just random subjects that had appealed to her. There was a portrait of Axel in her bedroom. She talked to it sometimes. He looked so alive and was smiling in the portrait. It made her happy, not sad. There was one of Jean-Louis in the living room, which showed his serious, pensive side. He had been twenty-eight when she painted the portrait shortly before he died. He looked like a boy to her now, at forty-two.

She showered and put on jeans and a soft pale blue sweater and stood at her easel. She added another coat of the underlayer, and made some notes. The subject was coming to a sitting that afternoon. She could hardly wait to get started, as she smiled and got to work.

Chapter 2

Charles Taylor went to his father's office at the bank the day after the funeral. The interment had been brief and grim. The reception at his father's house had been exhausting. Charles had spent the night there, since he wanted to be in the city early the next day. Faye had gone back to Atherton with Liam. Charles had been deep in conversation with a member of the board and didn't see them leave. They knew better than to bother him when he was talking business. Charlie had a single-track mode of operation, so they left. Liam was eager to leave and meet up with friends.

Charles was surprised by how well he slept in his father's house. He didn't feel his presence or sense any message from him. They had run out of things to say to each other years before and Charles had become an expert at deflecting his father's never-wavering criticism of his life choices and decisions. It had fallen on deaf ears for years. Patrick Taylor wasn't a kind man. Charlie hoped that he was himself, and tried to be. At worst, he was honest to the point of bluntness sometimes, in a casual, well-meaning way, which occasionally wounded its object more than he intended. He apologized when he was wrong or hurt someone's feelings. Charlie had a laser-beam, astute, all-seeing point of view. He could be cutting when he was angry. He had a temper, which didn't surface often and was quick to cool when it did. He hated laziness and dishonesty, and was merciless with either. He was an honest man, and expected the same from others. His words were sharp and intended to hurt if he felt betrayed, cheated, or disrespected. He was the commander of whatever ship he was on, and didn't tolerate mutiny, from inferiors or superiors alike. Charlie liked to be in control and get his own way, but he was honest and fair, and a man of integrity.

Liam never challenged his father's authority. He just did what he wanted, and counted on no one noticing, which was usually the case, since his parents were busy. He was a good kid. He never got in trouble in school, and got fabulous grades. He was as smart as his parents and sensible most of the time, with the occasional youthful poor judgment and foolishness, but not to excess. His parents were lucky. With very little supervision, Liam rarely caused a problem.

As Charlie walked around his father's home, he felt free. No one was going to criticize him, challenge him, put him down. He could breathe. The quarrelsome old man who had hounded him all his life was gone. Finally. Charlie wouldn't miss him.

Charlie informed the employees that he would be putting the house on the market soon and wanted any necessary small repairs taken care of immediately. They knew it was coming, and that

The Portrait

Charlie and his family wouldn't move to the city. Their house in Atherton was spectacular, and his father's was somewhat gloomy with dark wood paneling everywhere, and heavy drapes that kept out the sun and light. It was a beautiful home, but not for a young family. It looked like an English men's club, with a library filled with leather-bound books and first editions Patrick had collected. Charlie stood at the window for a minute, looking out at the view of the bay, and felt like his father as he stood there. It made him uncomfortable. He was the opposite of his father, intentionally.

He left for the bank after a cup of coffee in the kitchen. They had used the formal dining room for the reception the night before, its vitrines filled with antique silver.

The board members were waiting for Charlie in the boardroom at the bank and gave him a warm welcome. They stood up when he came into the room, to show respect, and he waved them to their seats, and took his own at the head of the table. A secretary he didn't know set down a cup of coffee for him. All of the board members had been at the funeral, the male members as pallbearers. Charlie tried not to think of it. There was no one Charlie's age on the board. They were all north of sixty, and most of them in their seventies, although capable, experienced, and alert. This was an informal gathering to welcome him.

One of the two women on the board, Mrs. Baker, the elderly widow, pointed to the large portraits of Charlie's father, grandfather, and great-grandfather, and smiled at him.

"We want one of you up there now," she said in a grandmotherly tone. "You have to sit for a portrait," she told him, and Charlie shook his head.

"I hate portraits," he said firmly. There was another one of Patrick at the house, in the library. Charlie had always hated it. His father looked pompous. "I don't sit anywhere long enough to be painted. I'll give you a photograph, you can put it on a table somewhere," he said, "or in a drawer."

"No," she insisted. "You need to pick an artist, and get a portrait done. You're the chairman of the board now. We'll give you till Christmas to do it." She spoke to him as though he were a child. Charlie ignored her and they chatted about a few minor items of business. They wanted to have the lobby of the bank painted over the summer. It was a big job and it would be expensive. Charlie approved it, and half an hour later, he thanked them and left. Mrs. Baker reminded him about the portrait as he was leaving. He had no intention of sitting for a portrait. The whole idea sounded absurd and arrogant to him. They had set the date for the next meeting.

He drove to his office in Palo Alto then. It was the opposite of his father's house and the offices at the bank. Everything in Charles's offices was white or beige, open and airy with light everywhere, and spectacular contemporary art. The two offices were as different as Charles and his father. Patrick had been the staunch defender of ancient traditions. Charlie had been breaking the sound barrier for his entire career.

He signed some papers, gathered up some materials for his trip, and then went home to his beautiful, splendidly decorated home in Atherton. Faye was at her office. He knew she was planning to work late, as she always did, and he wouldn't see her before he left. He hadn't said goodbye to her the night before when she left

The Portrait

the reception. It wasn't unusual for them in their disconnected life. He would see her in three weeks, and if some major problem came up while he was traveling, she'd call him on his cell. She never called him just to chat, nor did he call her.

Charlie crossed Liam in the hall at the house and they chatted for a minute. Liam was leaving the next day, excited to be going to Europe.

"Do you have enough money, euros, your credit card?" Charlie asked him, and Liam smiled. He'd been to Europe alone before.

"Mom's secretary got me everything I need," Liam said.

"Have a good trip," Charlie said and hugged him, and went to pack.

At five o'clock that afternoon, Charlie left for the airport. Liam had gone out by then. The house was silent when he locked the door and set the alarm. It was an odd feeling knowing how separate their lives were, but it had been that way for a long time. He wouldn't see Liam until he got back from Europe in August. He didn't even know his itinerary, but he knew that Faye would, or more precisely her secretary, Zina, who knew more about Liam's whereabouts at all times than either of his parents. He would see Faye when he got back in three weeks. Charlie didn't call her to say goodbye. She'd be in a meeting anyway, or on a conference call.

Charlie made it to the airport in half an hour, at full speed in his Aston Martin. He pulled into the part of the airport that was set aside for private planes.

The crew were waiting for him to come onboard, and they took off moments later, after they did their final checks. Charlie always cut it close, and the flight attendant brought him a drink once they were in the air. He chatted with her for a few minutes, and relaxed. It had been an easy day. He'd had the trip planned for a while, to check on the restaurants he wanted to buy. As part of the deal he was getting six that he didn't want, but there were twenty that he did. He had already negotiated the price. He wanted to see the restaurants in person before he signed the contract. Conveniently, his father's death and funeral hadn't derailed the trip.

He worked for a while on the plane, had a meal, slept, and went over the papers in his briefcase when he woke up, to make sure he had all the details fresh in his mind for the meeting the next day.

The private plane made Charlie's travel easier and more convenient. His father had been critical of that too, saying it was a frivolous expense and a luxury he didn't need, that it just made him look like a spoiled rich boy, and that the people Charlie did business with would disapprove. It was pointless to explain to Patrick that most of the people Charlie did business with had planes too. Charlie spent most of his time on the road, checking out restaurants and construction sites, meeting people to close deals all across the country. He worked at a brisk pace in a fast-moving world. He didn't have time to waste, and neither did his associates, or the people Charlie structured deals with.

The plane landed at Teterboro Airport in New Jersey slightly ahead of schedule. It had been a smooth flight. There were often storm warnings in the Midwest at that time of year, but there had been none that night. They taxied down the runway and took their assigned spot among a sea of private jets. It was the airport they all used. It was simpler than JFK, where they could be assigned a holding pattern for several hours while the big commercial flights came in from all over the world.

There was an SUV with a driver to pick Charlie up. He used a car service in New York, and he told the pilot and copilot he would see them in two days. They had his itinerary. His office was efficient. Charlie got into the car, and an hour later, they were at his address on Fifth Avenue in the heart of midtown, three blocks from Central Park.

Charlie loved coming to New York, the excitement and electricity of it. It was a far cry from his peaceful home in Atherton, and his office in Palo Alto. He did big business there, and was part of a club of high-tech titans who contributed to the success of the economy. But going to New York was like going to Mecca. It felt like the heartbeat of the universe, the whole city throbbing with its own special energy. It was dizzying in a way that he loved. Every fiber of his being was awake and alert, despite the late hour. It was three A.M. when he let himself into his apartment. It wasn't a home, it was a place to stay when he did business in New York. It was on the sixtieth floor, with a terrace. He dropped his bag in his bedroom and unlocked the doors to the terrace. A housekeeping service kept the place neat and clean in his absence. Gardeners had turned the terrace into a garden, where he could sit and relax on warm nights, with a dining table. He was wide-awake. It was only midnight in California, and he had slept on the flight. New York fueled and energized him and he was always a little bit sorry that he didn't come there more often. He had work all over the country.

He opened a bottle of chilled white wine, poured himself a

glass, and went out to lie in one of the comfortable deck chairs. He looked up at the sky and could see the stars. He sipped the wine and was the master of his world.

He used to come into the city when he was at Princeton, and he had longed to live there one day, but his father had wanted him to come straight back to California as soon as he graduated from business school and he never got the chance. He had always found the East more exciting, and would have liked to be part of it. He had had five years at Princeton, and three at Harvard. He had liked Boston, but nothing had the white-hot sizzle of New York. He was happy to be there, even if only for two days.

He gave himself half an hour to unwind, showered, and went to bed, and Ted Baker called him at eight o'clock the next morning. Charlie was drinking a cup of coffee, reading *The New York Times* on his iPad, and had been admiring the morning skyline. There was a steely beauty to it. He had done some deals with Ted Baker, and Ted had a new deal he wanted to discuss with him. Charlie had agreed to have dinner with him that night and listen to what he had in mind. They had been at business school together. Ted had made a name for himself with medical startups, and although he hadn't done quite as well as Charlie, he was a straight shooter and Charlie liked him.

"Are we still on for tonight?" Ted asked him when Charlie answered his phone.

"Of course. I'm going to be all over the place today, looking at restaurants, but I should be back in the city and ready to roll by seven."

"Sounds good. I'll reserve somewhere." They were both steak

The Portrait

and martini men, and had done some heavy drinking together in Cambridge in grad school. Ted was recently divorced, with three kids in Connecticut with his ex-wife, and having fun being on the single scene again. Charlie couldn't imagine what that would be like at nearly fifty, but the last time they had spoken, Ted said he was enjoying it. "I want to make a quick stop on the way to dinner, you can come with me. It's an art opening at a big deal gallery. I've seen the artist's work and it'll knock your socks off. Incredible portraits. I want to see the exhibit, and the opening is tonight. They give good parties, with lots of good-looking women." Charlie groaned when he said the word "portraits."

"Don't tell me you're going to have a portrait done."

"Not now. But you're no one in this town if you haven't had a Devon Darcy portrait done. They're amazing." Charlie couldn't tell if the artist was a man or a woman and didn't care.

"I'm chairman of the board of my father's bank now, and the board tried to talk me into having a portrait done to hang at the bank with the rogues' gallery of my ancestors."

"Terrific. You can check them out tonight."

"I'm planning to send the board a selfie. I'd feel a hundred years old having my portrait done. I'm never going to sit for a portrait, but I'm happy to go with you. I can vet the women for you while you look at the art. Or I can just hand out slips of paper with your number."

"I'm doing fine without your help, Taylor. I can check out the women *and* look at the art. I'll pick you up at your place at seven. Happy to see you, Charlie, and I think you'll like the deal I have my eye on."

"We can talk about it at dinner. See you later." Charlie was smiling when he hung up. He and Ted had had some good times together in Boston and New York twenty-five years before. He'd been dating Faye by then, and Ted thought he was crazy when he came back married from a Vegas weekend. Ted thought Faye was good-looking, but he knew that Charlie wasn't madly in love with her, and he could never understand why they had stayed married. He had never known two people who had less in common. Ted had been crazy in love with his wife when he married her, and now he was divorced, and Charlie was still married to the same woman, a marriage Ted had thought would never work.

By nine A.M., Charlie was in the car, being driven to all the locations on his list, in the five boroughs of New York, and several farther out of the city. He had a busy day, but it helped him decide which restaurants he would keep and which he would sell—there were several that he really wanted, though he had to buy all twenty of them to get the choice ones.

At the end of the day, when he got back to the hotel, Charlie showered, shaved, and changed into a perfectly cut summer-weight dark blue suit that his New York tailor had made for him. He looked sensational in the dark suit with his dark hair. He was a handsome man.

Charlie went downstairs and stood on the sidewalk, enjoying the hustle and bustle on the streets, watching people, and keeping an eye out for Ted. Charlie mildly envied him his new bachelor life, but he was sure there was a downside to it too, which was why he and Faye had decided not to divorce. The divorce must have cost Ted a fortune, and he knew he'd given his ex the house,

The Portrait

a big sprawling mansion in Greenwich, because his children had grown up there, and his wife still lived there. Charlie had never liked Emily much when they were all in grad school together. Faye had been a lot more fun, and even that had faded within a year of their marriage. They weren't kids anymore, and the last time he'd seen Emily, she had let her hair go gray and gained some weight. It wasn't a good look. She was two years younger than Faye, and looked a lot older.

Ted showed up five minutes late, driving a silver Ferrari. He honked and waved at Charlie, who ran around the car and got in. He glanced over at Ted as he took off down Fifth Avenue, made a left, and headed east, and then turned up Madison, heading uptown.

Charlie glanced at him with a grin. "Nice car. Part of your seduction act?" Charlie teased him.

"I just got it," Ted said proudly. "And I don't need a car to close the deal."

"Lucky for you," Charlie quipped, as they headed uptown on Madison Avenue, past all the restaurants and elegant shops.

"What's new on the home front? Liam okay?"

"Better than ever. He just graduated from Yale last month, and is going back for grad school after the summer, to study architecture. He's leaving for Europe today, to check out some châteaux in France, and castles in England."

"He sounds a lot better behaved and smarter than we were," Ted said with a smile. "Thanks for indulging me, so we can see the opening of that show tonight. I'm mesmerized by those portraits. When I know I've made it, I'm going to sit for one, and then I'll know I've really arrived." Charlie laughed at the reverent way he said it, as though the artist was some kind of sacred status symbol. Ted spoke of the work in a tone of awe, which seemed odd to Charlie and surprised him. They made small talk about mutual friends on the drive uptown. Ted was in touch with more of their classmates than Charlie, since most of them lived in and around New York, and fewer had landed in the West.

The gallery was impressive, and Charlie recognized the name when they got there. They handled important artists, and a valet parker took the car. A number of people were leaving, and stood on the sidewalk talking, waiting for their cars, or just chatting before they left, as Ted and Charlie headed toward a knot of people at the door. They could see through the windows that there was still a big crowd inside. Charlie smiled, the scene was so typically New York. There was a lot of security on the sidewalk, and someone said that both the mayor and the governor were there.

As Ted and Charlie tried to make their way into the gallery, there was a tangle of humanity blocking the door, trying to make their way out. Their bodies were pressed together and nothing moved for a minute, as Ted and Charlie tried to inch sideways through the crowd, with others ahead of and behind them. Charlie smelled her faint exotic Oriental perfume before he saw her. It was a musky scent of patchouli with a dash of spice which caught his attention, and was an extremely pleasant sensation. There was a mysterious quality to it, and he wondered which of the women around him was wearing it. There was a mass of red hair next to him, so close he could have touched it, as he smelled the perfume. The head turned then, and Charlie held his breath for an instant

The Portrait

when he saw her. She had an exquisite delicate face, creamy white skin, and piercing green eyes, the color of Imperial jade. She was looking directly at him, and the world stopped for an instant. Some overpowering force made him want to touch her face, and she gave him the smallest of smiles, as though they were intended to meet and she was pleased to see him. They were crushed against each other, and he felt an electric current run through him as the logjam tightened around them and seemed to bring her even closer. She was less solidly on her feet than Charlie to withstand the crowd. He was taller and stronger. She was wearing a black dress and jacket, and what mesmerized him were her remarkable green eyes. He noticed that she had graceful hands and wore no rings.

"I'm sorry," he said softly, just loud enough for her to hear him, and she nodded, and an instant later, the knot loosened and she was propelled forward away from him, and all he could see when he looked was her back and her red hair. He felt an almost irresistible compulsion to follow her, but she was nearly through the door by then. She didn't turn to look at him, but he stared at her, and found himself deposited into the main gallery with the rest of the people arriving. The paintings around him were incredible. The show was beautiful. He spotted the governor, and he realized that two of the portrait subjects were standing near him. He recognized them immediately, standing near their portraits, looking proud.

There was an alcove of children's portraits that were poignant. The artist had an incredible gift. Each portrait looked as though it was about to speak and tell a deep secret. There had obviously been a powerful bond between the subjects and the artist. Each portrait told you something intimate and personal about the subject.

A group of museum directors were speaking to the gallery owner, among them the director of the Metropolitan Museum. Two of them wanted to purchase Devon's work. Charlie could see from the red dots next to every painting that an hour after the show had opened, all of the paintings had been sold. Probably several even before that. The commissions were purchased, obviously, but so were all the paintings of children in the room of random subjects. Devon had been very happy when she left. Six commissions had been requested. The show was a resounding success.

Charlie felt breathless as he toured the gallery to see all the paintings. There were portraits of two famous women, while all the others were of men. Ted found Charlie as he stood looking at one of the portraits. They had a fresh contemporary feel to them, but had been painted in a classical style. She had a method all her own, with a kind of magic to it. It was that same compelling feeling of deep mystery, love and long-hidden pain, and raw emotion that he had seen in the redheaded woman's eyes on the way in. She had seemed powerful and fragile at the same time. He felt haunted by her now.

"The paintings are something else, aren't they?" Ted said when he found him. It was almost a religious experience looking at the art. Her talent exploded off the canvas with a life force that held you in its grip, and you couldn't tear yourself away from the paintings. Charlie turned to Ted with a look of amazement. Some of the

The Portrait

paintings of the children made him want to cry, they were so touching and alive, full of innocence and joy yet with a hint of sadness. Devon brought everything she had lived and experienced into her art.

"The paintings are amazing," Charlie said, feeling dazed and awestruck.

"I think we passed the artist on our way in," Ted said vaguely. "The woman with the red hair, if you noticed her. There's a picture of her on the gallery director's desk."

Before they left, Charlie went to the desk and picked up one of the folders set there for the guests to take. There were photographs of several of the paintings in it, most of them of famous subjects anyone would recognize, and a list of the people the artist had painted. The prices for her portrait sittings were listed as "upon request," depending on the size, which didn't surprise him. He was sure they were appropriately steep. As he looked at them, Charlie thought of the portrait the board wanted of him to hang in the boardroom. The paintings he was looking at were entirely different from the stuffy, pompous portraits of his ancestors, but they had so much more meaning—they were a collaboration between the artist and the subject, a secret they had shared, a moment of communion that would last forever in the portrait. He had felt that bond himself for a minute when he saw her. She was a woman without artifice, without armor or a shell. She looked at you from the depths of her soul, and looked straight into yours with those powerful green eyes at once strong and gentle. She was from another world. She seemed like a woman who could do no harm, but perhaps had been injured herself, and turned the wound into a blessing through her art. Ted would have liked to have a portrait painted by her as a symbol of his success. Charlie would have liked to sit for a portrait with her so he could see her again. He was still haunted by her as they left the show. Ted had made a point of meeting the governor and the mayor. Charlie didn't care about them. The only person he would have wanted to meet was the artist. He spoke to no one while he was there, he was too intent on the art. He took the folder with him, the valet collected Ted's car, and Charlie got in. He felt as though all the air had been knocked out of him.

"Thank you," he said to Ted. "They're the most beautiful paintings I've ever seen."

"It makes you want to have one, doesn't it?" Ted agreed as he drove them to the restaurant. "I'm sure I can't afford her, but you can." Charlie didn't believe in portraits. He always said that he thought they were a meaningless narcissistic gesture, because he associated the idea with his father and the portraits of him. But what Devon did was entirely different. It was true art that deserved to be in a museum, and would last for centuries, and the bond between her and her subject would still be there, as alive a hundred or two hundred years later as it was today.

"I don't think the boardroom at the bank deserves a work of art like that," Charlie said respectfully, as they reached the restaurant and got out of the car. He could hardly concentrate on the menu to order dinner. They both ordered burgers at the trendy restaurant, which was as crowded as the gallery had been.

Ted explained the deal he had in mind to Charlie, who didn't turn it down, but wasn't as enthused as Ted had hoped, and he

The Portrait

trusted his old friend's instincts. Charlie had an unfailing nose for what would work, and what would never be more than ordinary. He told Ted to keep him apprised of his progress, but he didn't leap to join him in the deal. Ted was disappointed but didn't press him. Charlie knew what he liked and what he didn't. And when something sparked for him he was relentless, pursuing it with passion and excitement. Ted's proposal just didn't turn him on, or make him want to join him.

They enjoyed the dinner together, and Charlie thanked him again for taking him to the show. He said it had been a wonderful experience. He still felt as though he hadn't come back to earth yet. The two men promised to stay in touch and get together again when Charlie next came to New York.

He put the gallery folder on his desk when he got home and walked out to his terrace, sat down in a lounge chair, and looked up at the sky, thinking about Devon, and when their eyes had met when they were pressed together in the crowd. She was so close he could have touched her face, her hair. The world had stopped turning when he looked at her. He couldn't breathe. All he could see was her. Everything around them was a silent blur. He wondered if all her subjects felt that way about her or if this was different. He had never felt anything like it. He was still haunted by her when he went to bed, and the only thing he knew was that he had to have a portrait painted by her, just so he could see her and talk to her. He didn't want to wait for a portrait. It was midnight by then, too late to call her. But he knew he had to speak to her and see her. He had to see those mysterious, magical green eyes again.

Chapter 3

Charlie thought about the evening before over breakfast, and how best to proceed. He called the gallery and told them who he was and that he wanted to meet the artist.

They told him everything from the show that was available had been sold. He asked her prices, which were very steep, almost shocking, but worth it. He said again that he wanted to meet her. They were noncommittal and said they'd get back to him. They were used to important people inquiring at the gallery about her work. They were respectful but not impressed, and called him back half an hour later, telling him that Devon was fully committed until the end of the year and she was not taking commissions for next year yet. He said he'd like to speak to her himself. They said she wasn't accepting calls. She was working. The more they refused him, the more determined he was to see her and talk to her. Charlie asked if they would deliver something to her, and they said of course, since they knew he was an important man. But they explained that Devon's rules were strict and they abided by them.

Charlie wrote her a note saying he saw her as she left the gallery, was bowled over by her work and would like to speak to her, and that he was only in New York for another day. He added that he would stretch it for her. She was rapidly becoming an obsession, which he didn't say but he could feel it overwhelming him. He felt breathless writing the note.

He dressed and left the apartment and walked to a florist five blocks away. He ordered a huge bouquet of flowers he picked himself to be delivered to the gallery, or her home if the gallery would tell them the address. He left an enormous tip, and walked back to his apartment. He had put his cell phone number on the letter to her. He had meetings all day and he worked at the apartment that night. He was surrounded by papers, charts, and his computer when his cellphone rang. It was Devon Darcy. Her voice was as soft as silk, and as powerful in its effect as the look in her eyes had been the night before.

"That's an enormous bouquet, Mr. Taylor," she said in a low, smooth voice. There was the hint of a smile in her tone. There was that same gentle strength about her.

"I'm glad it got to you. I was afraid it wouldn't," Charlie said, feeling shaken when he heard her voice, which was as delicate and sensual as her face and her perfume.

"The gallery is very good about getting things to me. The flowers are beautiful," she said, sounding shy.

"I love your work," he said, his voice was gentle, yet masculine and strong. "Your paintings are incredible."

The Portrait

"I love doing my work." She sounded happy when she said it.

"I need a portrait," he said simply. Suddenly it seemed crucial, and urgent. "Would you have coffee with me?" he asked her. He wanted to see her again to determine if she was as mysterious and beautiful as he remembered. Maybe it was just an illusion with a fleeting glance—they had crossed paths so quickly. Maybe he had imagined the electricity between them.

She hesitated. "I can't. I'm working. I've just started a portrait. I don't see people when I'm painting. I'm fully booked through December, and I haven't started booking for next year." His invitation felt more like a date than a commission, and she had too much work lined up to be frivolous. She was always serious about her work. It was her priority, as his work was his.

"Just have coffee with me." He sounded so persuasive. She wondered why. "Half an hour. I promise I won't keep you longer." There was something so sensual and appealing about his voice, both soft and strong. She could tell he was a man who was used to getting his way. She wasn't sure why, but she succumbed to his persistent charm. Normally, she never saw anyone but her subject when she painted.

"Half an hour," she said firmly. "An hour at most."

"Where?" His heart was beating faster, and he felt like a boy again. She gave him the name of a café he'd never heard of in the Village.

"Tomorrow. Does five P.M. work for you?" she asked him politely. The sitting would be over by then. He wanted to ask her for dinner, but he didn't dare. He was sure she wouldn't accept. He already knew after talking to her that he wanted her to do his portrait, and wondered what it would take to convince her. He had to extend his stay in New York by a day to see her and change a meeting in Chicago, but he did it gladly to meet with her. Normally, he'd have expected her to adjust to his schedule, but he was certain she wouldn't. She was hesitant about seeing him and could have refused to meet him.

"Five is great, at Luigi's café," he confirmed. It sounded like an adventure to him. He was excited at the prospect and his spirits soared. It was like winning a prize to have gotten the appointment with her.

"See you then, Mr. Taylor, and thank you again for the flowers," she said formally, with just a hint of irony in her tone.

"Charlie," he corrected her.

"See you tomorrow," she said in her soft voice, and hung up.

Charlie sat holding the phone in his hand after she ended the call. He was staring into space, thinking about her, remembering her voice, wondering what it would be like meeting her, talking to her. She seemed so mysterious right now, so talented, so far away, and yet when he heard her voice she felt as close to him as she had in the crowd. He couldn't figure out who she was, or why she had such a powerful effect on him. Maybe he was imagining it, and she was just an ordinary person. But the paintings she created were anything but ordinary. They were the work of a fascinating, very unusual woman. He wanted to know her better, and was grateful she had agreed to meet him. When he didn't hear from her all day after he sent the flowers, he had been sure she wouldn't see him. Her call that night had been a surprise and a gift.

He had trouble sleeping that night, and kept dreaming about

The Portrait

her. He would wake up with a start when she vanished in the dream. He finally fell into a deep dreamless sleep for the last hour and woke up with a feeling of excitement. Knowing he was going to see her energized him. He organized a meeting to fill the time that day until he saw her, and he could barely keep his mind on the subject. It was a relief when he finally got into the car at four o'clock to go downtown to meet her. There was heavy traffic on the way, as he gazed out the window, thinking of her.

In spite of the traffic, Charlie got to the café in the Village ten minutes early. It had a European-style terrace, lively, busy, crowded. It had taken him nearly an hour to get there in the end-of-day traffic from his apartment. He was wearing a gray business suit and blue shirt, open at the neck, without the tie he'd worn that day to the meeting he'd arranged to make use of the extra day in town.

Charlie had a thick head of dark hair, and his shoulders looked broad in the custom-made shirt. He took off the jacket while he waited. The terrace was crowded, the waiters were busy, the day was warm. It felt more like Paris or Rome than New York.

Devon arrived at precisely five o'clock, in a white T-shirt, jeans, and black ballet flats. Her hair shone like copper in the sun. He had texted her a description of what he looked like to the number she'd called from the night before. She had done the same, once she got his text, but he knew exactly what she looked like. He couldn't get her out of his mind. She had the slim body of a young girl, the posture of a dancer—she was shorter than he remembered and must have been wearing heels at the opening of her show.

She remembered him immediately and sat down next to him at the table. He could smell the exotic perfume she'd worn before. He exuded the same magnetic pull she had felt in the crowd when she saw him. There was something powerful within him, mirrored by the strength in her. He ordered a glass of white wine, and she a glass of lemonade. "I don't drink when I'm working," she explained. The people around them were fun to watch, like a scene in a movie. There was something unreal about meeting her. It was all so unexpected and atypical of his daily life, meeting an artist to paint his portrait.

"You don't look American," he commented, mesmerized by her green eyes and red hair. Her eyes were a deep true green, with the translucence of emeralds, just as he remembered. His were a striking blue.

"I am American," she confirmed. "Born in New York. I lived here until I was five. My parents died then. My mother was French so I went to live with my grandmother in France, and stayed there until I was twenty-eight. I came back here to live fourteen years ago." He rapidly did the math, and was surprised by her age. She looked so much younger. She made it all sound so simple, and didn't say that she left France and came back to New York because Axel had died. She felt private about it. Axel belonged to her.

"You look French," he said, admiring her, as they sipped their drinks. Even in a white T-shirt and jeans, she had a distinctive style. She had looked chic at the gallery, the night before. He liked seeing her informally in the T-shirt and jeans.

"Why do you want a portrait?" she asked, watching him closely. He explained about his father and the bank, and the board. She

The Portrait

didn't object and nodded. She was used to commissions for purposes like that.

"Do you have children?" he asked her, wanting to know more about her as a person.

"No, I don't," she said quietly. She didn't want to share Axel with him. It was a business meeting, despite the current and attraction she felt. "I could book you in January," she offered. He intrigued her. There was something so strong and determined about him. "Do you have children?" she asked him. She wondered if he was married. He didn't seem like it, and wore no ring. He had stopped wearing it a year after he married Faye. She no longer wore hers either. Neither of them cared. The symbol it represented had become meaningless to both of them over the years.

"I have a son. He left for Paris yesterday. He's going to study architecture at grad school at Yale in the fall."

They talked about Paris and San Francisco, the Beaux-Arts and Harvard. He told her what he did, which told her he was a money man. It wasn't a glamorous business, but surely lucrative. He made her think of fire and ice. She wondered what it would be like to paint him, and if he would open up, or hide who he really was, if he would be bold or vulnerable. She wasn't sure. She could sense that he was both. She had the feeling that he was hiding from himself, or from something. She studied people carefully and paid attention. She was quiet as she watched him, and he was fascinated by her. She was so beautiful and so modest. Now that he had seen her paintings he was profoundly impressed by her and the magnitude of her talent.

"Can I walk you home?" he asked her when they stood up. She

made him feel boyish again. When they got to her house, she stopped and thanked him for the lemonade. She was smiling and had enjoyed the time with him, even more than she'd expected to.

"See you in January," she said lightly when he left her outside her house.

"If you get an opening before that, I'll rearrange my schedule," he said with a pleading look. She had explained that she worked from videos and photographs she took at the first session, for people who lived far away.

She wished him a good summer, then floated up the stairs with a light step, unlocked the outer door, waved, and disappeared, her red hair a burst of flame as she went through the door.

Charlie walked all the way back to his apartment, miles from where she lived. She had stayed for two hours, not one, and he was more intrigued by her than ever and didn't want to wait seven months to see her again. If anything, he was more obsessed with her than before. There was something so haunting and mysterious about her, so fragile and yet so powerful.

She had asked him interesting questions that would help her when she painted him. She was already studying the angles of his face while he talked to her. She thought there was more to him than what he allowed anyone to see. She guessed that he was good at hiding his emotions, and that when anyone came too close to him, he made light of it or fled. He appeared to be open and straightforward but she could already sense that Charlie never let anyone see his more intimate side. She had a feeling that he had been hurt, she didn't know by what, but he protected himself and kept people at arm's length while appearing not to. She had a sixth

The Portrait

sense for people, and the electric current that ran between them made her feel closer to him than she usually did to her subjects at first. She had a natural reserve, mixed with shyness, but she felt surprisingly comfortable with him as she drank her lemonade, and when he walked her home afterward.

He had talked about his son, but he didn't say if he was married. She assumed he wasn't, or he would have mentioned his wife then. Most people did when you met them, as a subtle way of sharing their status. He said he had lived in the East for thirteen years, for boarding school, college, and grad school, and a gap year running his first startup between college and business school, but he had returned to the West immediately after business school, to take his place in Silicon Valley and get to work. And he said he still loved visiting New York. He loved the energy and how engaged people were in exciting activities. She said she loved it too, and how many creative people there were. They had talked about Paris, another of his favorite cities. They had covered a lot of ground in two hours. She didn't talk about the people she had painted, and he respected how discreet she was. She was modest to the point of humble, in spite of her enormous talent. It was obvious how much she loved her work.

She had noticed how his eyes clouded when he talked about his father, and why he wanted the portrait. She was shocked to realize that his father had died only days before.

"You must be mourning him," she had said, instantly sympathetic, and he thought about it for a minute, wanting to be honest with her. If she was going to paint him, she deserved to know who he was, and what was true about him. He thought he owed the naked truth. He didn't hide who he was from her. She was easy to open up to, warm and kind.

"Actually, I'm not mourning him. We never got along. He was a harsh man. He expected a lot. I was never the son he hoped I would be. I suppose it would be fair to say that we never understood each other. I tried for a while when I was young. The only way he could accept was his own. There was no other way with him. We were diametrically different. I don't think he even liked me." He looked sad when he said it. He seemed so open and unguarded for a moment that she wanted to reach out and touch him, but she didn't.

"And your mother?" she asked gently.

"She died when I was thirteen. My father sent me away to school a few months later, and I never really came home again. Thirteen is too young to leave home. I made the same mistake with my own son. I let him go to boarding school too soon. He wanted to, as an only child. He wanted to be with other kids, and my wife was a big fan of boarding school. I wasn't. The only thing I liked about it was escaping my father. I was homesick for the first two years. By the time I was sixteen, I actually enjoyed it. And then I was off and running. You grow up faster away from home, especially with no parents." Devon was easy to say hard things to, that he never said to anyone else.

"I don't remember my parents," Devon had said quietly. "I was five when they died. Once in a while, I think I have a memory, but I think it's probably something my grandmother must have told me. I don't actually remember it myself. My grandmother brought me up from five to sixteen. She was tough but wonderful. She was

The Portrait

very strict, but she made it possible for me to go to the Beaux-Arts. She worked hard and saved the money for it, and left it to me."

"It seems like a very good investment." He smiled at her, and she smiled back at him. She had a beautiful smile and sensuous lips. If he had lost control of himself, he would have wanted to kiss her.

Charlie remembered all of it when he sat on his terrace, playing it all over in his head. The time he had spent with her was like a movie he wanted to see again. He hated the thought of waiting seven months to see her, and he was sure that he wouldn't get bumped up on her waiting list. No one would cancel. He would just have to wait.

He slept easily that night, and woke up refreshed the next morning. He was flying out that day.

He sent Devon a text before he did. He was on his way to the airport when he sent it. "Thank you for seeing me yesterday. It meant the world to me." He was intrigued by everything he had learned about her, and had seen for himself, while they sat at Luigi's, exposing parts of their lives to each other, like a chess game they were playing, but it was real life. Her early life had been more difficult than his. Charlie had had every advantage in his life, but he had had a loveless childhood. There was no one to love and comfort him, which was the cruelest fate of all, as Devon knew only too well. She had been alone for so many years. There had been a brief moment of true happiness with Jean-Louis and Axel, but it ended all too quickly. And even with what he knew about her childhood now, Charlie didn't see her as a tragic figure. She had too much fire and passion in her to seem that way to him. She looked peaceful and happy when she spoke of her grandmother. There had been no fairy grandmother in Charlie's early life. There had literally been no one to love him. His childhood had been far more tragic than Devon's, although most people wouldn't have seen it that way. She did.

And she had told him just enough about herself to tantalize him and fascinate him even more. She had given him a lot to think about for the next seven months. It was all engraved in his mind now, along with her exquisite face and incredible all-seeing green eyes.

He thought about her as he sat on the plane, waiting to take off for Chicago. Right before the plane taxied down the runway, she answered his text, and he smiled as he read it.

"I'm looking forward to January." That was all she said, followed by the initials DD. It was a start. She had just validated everything they had said and shared the day before.

Charlie completed everything he had to do on his travels, and he hit the ground running when he got back to San Francisco. He met with the two best realtors in the city to show them his father's house and get an idea about the price he should put on it. Both came up with big numbers. It was a beautiful home, built by a famous architect. It was well maintained, in surprisingly good condition, with some modernizations that were direly necessary, to replace kitchens and bathrooms. A new owner would want to do that themselves, so Charlie didn't make any major improvements. He drove up to Lake Tahoe on the weekend to meet a realtor and

The Portrait

do the same at his father's house there. In both homes he picked the things he wanted to keep in storage, some valuable furniture, a few paintings he wanted. A portrait of his mother in their city dining room, and one of his father. He didn't want to get rid of them, Liam might want them one day. Charlie thought about putting the portrait of his mother in his own house, but decided it would make him too sad to see her every day. She was a gentle memory now, and he preferred to keep it that way.

He selected expensive items he didn't want to keep and preferred to sell at auction, and had his assistant arrange to ship them to Sotheby's in New York.

He ran into Faye in the kitchen the afternoon he came back from Tahoe. It had been a long day. He didn't see her until he'd been home from his trip for several days. Once they gave up the pretense of sleeping together, they had bedrooms at opposite ends of the house. They'd both been out a lot that week, and their schedules were different. He came home late after business dinners, she went to bed early after long hours at the office. She rose hours before he did for the gym or early yoga classes. She was usually out by the time he reached the kitchen for coffee.

He had made a list of things she might want from the Tahoe house. He showed it to her and she declined them all. He was bringing all of his father's crystal, silver, and fine china to the house in Atherton. He had no idea where to put it—their cupboards were all full—but he didn't want to send it to storage.

"What kind of shape is the house in?" Faye asked him. She hated his father's Tahoe house and hadn't been there in ten years. It had always depressed her and she had no intention of ever going back there again. She had her own mountain home in Aspen and had owned it for a decade. When she acknowledged to herself that she and Charlie would never be a real couple again, she bought a house in a place she loved, with enough bedrooms for their son to visit from time to time, and to entertain her friends. She wanted to use it for vacations by herself, and the occasional weekend.

She loved Aspen, had researched the house market carefully, and found just the one she wanted. It was in easy walking distance from the heart of town, if she didn't want to take her car out. In the ten years she'd owned it, Liam had been there a few times, and Charlie twice. Liam was an avid skier, but he had come in summer too. It was a peaceful, happy place for her. It was just the right balance of natural beauty and rural sophistication, which described her masterfully. It was Faye's favorite place to be, and she was safe from any intrusion on Charlie's part, since the altitude made him sick every time he was there, and gave him headaches and nightmares. She had bought the house with no intention of sharing it with him. It was her personal retreat, which he respected.

"The house is in decent shape, but old," he said of his father's house. "The new owners will want to remodel it and modernize it. It seems a little sad right now," which didn't surprise either of them.

They chatted for a few minutes longer.

"What have you been up to?" he asked her. They intersected like housemates and old friends. They didn't even argue much anymore. They were cordial, polite, and distant. There had been endless heated battles, before they'd given up all illusions about it being a viable marriage.

"I'm packing. I leave tomorrow." She smiled at him.

"Aspen?"

"Of course." It made her happy just thinking about it. She spent six to eight weeks there in the summer, and worked remotely. She went hiking in the mountains, rode horses, and enjoyed the cultural aspects offered there every summer, and the skiing in winter. Buying the house in Aspen had been one of the best things she'd ever done for herself. "How was your trip?" she asked him.

"Long, busy, interesting. The board at the bank wants me to have a portrait done. I met an artist I want to do it," he said, feeling a little foolish.

"That's a new twist. It doesn't sound like you." Faye was surprised.

"It isn't, but she's a terrific artist. I think it'll be great." Faye went back to her packing then. He was leaving in a few days too.

Charlie rented the same house in East Hampton every summer. He loved the sea. It was a beautiful old New England-style home on the beach, owned by a family who no longer used it but wanted to keep it. He kept a sailboat there that he could sail alone. It was a magnificent wood boat. Faye got seasick just looking at boats. Once in a while they laughed about how incompatible they were. They were a textbook case.

Faye marveled at the fact that they were still married after twenty-three years. They hadn't vacationed together in a dozen years. Their last attempts to do so had been disastrous. Liam was ten and they had argued constantly. After that, they sent Liam to camp for two months in the summer and vacationed separately.

"I don't know how we managed to have so much fun together

at Harvard," Faye had said to him once. "If we'd met on a game show, we'd have been disqualified in the first round."

"A lot of sex," Charlie answered her with a grin. "I don't think we ever talked to each other."

"Oh that," Faye said vaguely. They hadn't had sex with each other in ten years. It was a part of their relationship they had given up when they realized that their marriage was dead.

He didn't see her when she left for Aspen the next day. She left him a note about some house repairs her assistant had scheduled while she'd be away. Charlie was leaving for the Hamptons three days later.

He was wrapping up at his desk the afternoon before he left when Liam called. He was good about checking in. He'd been having a fantastic time, exploring châteaux and traveling with his friends. They had gone to Venice for a few days and loved it, and were back in France. They had stayed at a sixteenth-century palazzo that had been turned into a hotel.

It was five in the afternoon in California, and two A.M. in France, late for Liam to call, but he didn't sound drunk.

"What are you doing up at this hour?" his father asked him. When Liam answered, Charlie realized his voice sounded strained. He said they'd been walking in a forest somewhere in Normandy, he had stumbled over a tree root and had broken his ankle, and it hurt like hell. He was calling from the hospital, and sounded like a little kid. Charlie listened, and hesitated. "Did you call your

The Portrait

mother?" he asked him. Liam usually addressed medical issues to her. Charlie was better with work, travel, and school.

"Yeah, she has friends staying with her. She said to fly to Aspen and I can stay with her." Charlie knew Faye's reactions, and her theories about motherhood. Nurturing was not her strong suit. She had mistakenly believed that the parents' job was over when the kids turned eighteen and left for college. From what Charlie observed among his friends, the hard part only started then.

"I'll pick you up tomorrow," he said decisively. Instead of flying to New York, he would fly to Paris, pick Liam up, and take him to the Hamptons for as long as he wanted to stay. He'd enjoy having him there. He sounded like he was in pain. "Are you on crutches?"

"Yeah. I can't put my weight on it. They had to put a pin in it." Liam had been gone for four weeks, and was cutting his trip short by a few weeks, but he sounded ready to come home. It wasn't going to be fun traveling with a broken ankle. He had left time in his schedule to see his friends before he left for school, but it would be hard for him to get around now. It was his right ankle so he couldn't drive, which would be very inconvenient.

After he spoke to Liam, Charlie called his pilot and told him of the change of plan for the next day.

"I'll book a space at Le Bourget airport." It was where people kept their private planes. They would only get to the Hamptons a day late, and Charlie hoped that Liam would stay for a while. It would be a good chance to have some father-son time and catch up before Liam went back to Yale, and Charlie had no big plans for the moment. He tried to slow down for a few weeks in the summer to recharge his batteries. That way he could attack all his currently pending projects with new energy in the fall.

As Charlie had asked him to, Liam texted him when he got back to his hotel. His text told his father that he was safe and sound, and would try to sleep for a few hours. He was exhausted after the injury, the shock, and the anesthesia and surgery when they set his ankle. His friends had gone on to the next stop without him, and were visiting a little known château with splendid gardens in Normandy. Liam had told them his father was coming and he was leaving with him.

Liam was lying in bed when Charlie got there. One of the maids had brought him a sandwich on a baguette, and he was eating. His face broke into a broad smile when he saw his father and they hugged. Liam clung to him for a minute. It had been scary having surgery in a foreign country, and the pain had been agonizing. He had a knee-high orthopedic boot to wear for the next six weeks, in lieu of a cast, but at least he could take it off to shower or bathe, and eventually, when he could put weight on the ankle, walk into the ocean. Charlie believed in the healing powers of the sea.

Charlie helped him off the bed, and lent a hand while Liam gathered his things. They didn't spend time in the city at all. It was hard for Liam to get around on the crutches, and he was still in pain. They headed straight back to Le Bourget, where Charlie's relief crew were waiting for him, and they had already been given approval for their flight plan to New York. Charlie assisted Liam to the bedroom on the plane, helped him into bed, turned on the TV for him, and handed him the remote, which Liam took gratefully.

"Try to get some sleep," Charlie suggested gently. Liam was looking pale, and still shaken. Charlie brought him some food after takeoff, and Liam was already sound asleep. Charlie closed the door softly and went back to his seat. He had brought work to do on the flight. But once he got to the Hamptons, he never worked, except if there was a crisis somewhere in his business that required his attention. He needed time to unwind, and he was looking forward to spending time with Liam. It would be a rare treat for however long he stayed, even if only a few days, until he felt better. His parents' lack of attention to him growing up had made Liam independent. With kids that age, in their early twenties, Charlie had learned to be grateful for whatever time they got together. It was never enough now, but it was better than not seeing him at all. He loved his son and regretted the time he hadn't spent with him when he was younger. He tried to make up for it whenever he could. And he was happy to help him now. Liam slept for the entire flight, and his father woke him when they landed back at Teterboro.

A customs officer met them at the plane and cleared them. Charlie helped Liam into the waiting SUV, and they headed for the Hamptons. Liam looked better already after sleeping for the whole flight, and Charlie glanced at his son with fatherly pride. He was a good guy in spite of his parents' mistakes and inattention. He was grateful that Liam didn't seem to hold it against him.

Charlie couldn't wait to get to the house and see the ocean in East Hampton. He was glad that Liam had come with him. It made the broken ankle seem like an unexpected blessing, if it gave them some time together. Charlie was grateful to have a son like Liam. He was sensible and intelligent and kind. It made up for everything else. He knew he was a lucky man.

Chapter 4

The house in East Hampton was impeccable when Charlie arrived, as it was every year. It was a big, rambling family home, with many bedrooms, and a couple who lived there year-round and kept it in excellent repair. Charlie loved it and had tried several times to buy it from the owners. They had inherited it from their parents. They lived in Boston and had a house in Maine that they preferred. But they wanted to keep the house in the family for their children, and as an investment. Charlie was their only renter, and since their children were young teenagers, he figured that he was still good there for several years, and he hoped they would relent and change their minds eventually and sell it to him. The owners weren't part of the old-guard snobbish Hamptons social scene. They were avid sailors, and preferred the boating life in Maine. The Hamptons were the only place where Charlie got some respite from his intense business life and constant travel. He stopped everything when he stayed there every year. The owners had even let him stay there a few times in winter, when he was in New York and needed a break for a few days. He loved it in winter too. And he loved having Liam there with him now. He gave him a big sunny guest bedroom on the main floor, where the kitchen, dining room, two living rooms, a cozy den, and guest suites were located, so Liam didn't have to negotiate the stairs. Charlie's master suite was upstairs at one end of the house, with a charming balcony and a widow's walk, where he could see far out to sea. He stood there every morning, watching the ocean. He kept his beloved sailboat at a marina nearby, and left it there all year. Unlike his mother, Liam shared his father's love of sailboats, although it would be tricky getting him on the boat this year, with the broken ankle. Charlie doubted they could do it, and Liam couldn't walk on the beach, but there was plenty to do in the Hamptons, and they wouldn't be bored. There were restaurants and shops, places to explore. He had books to read, games to play, and Liam was good at entertaining himself with video games and his computer. Charlie was happy to be his chauffeur for the duration of his stay. There was a terrific bookstore in town, which Charlie always visited and where he bought a stack of current books he hadn't had the time to read.

The housekeeper was happy to cook for him, but he enjoyed cooking for himself, or dining at any of the very good restaurants while he was there. There was a very active social life in the Hamptons, which ranged from casual to formal dinner parties, but Charlie usually kept to himself, enjoying the downtime and the long walks on the magnificent white sand beach that stretched for miles.

The Portrait

The house had a decidedly New England feel to it. It wasn't showy, but it was solid, well kept, well laid out, and handsomely decorated in a restrained New England way. It reminded him of grand homes he had seen on Cape Cod when he was in college. It didn't have the lavish flash more typical of California, or the grandeur of some of the older estates in Southampton. Charlie didn't want to show off there, he just wanted to relax. He and Liam lived in shorts and T-shirts and bare feet. There was a large swimming pool the current owners had added when their parents died, and they were thinking of putting in a tennis court and had more than enough land to do it. The Hamptons were an interesting combination of beach and country. Most people seemed to treat the area as more of a country retreat, but what Charlie loved about it was the ocean. There were extensive lawns on the property, and Charlie frequently saw deer crossing them in broad daylight with their young. It was the only place where Charlie rested and felt at peace, other than on his sailboat. He loved working on his boat every year, and keeping it in perfect condition. He enjoyed maintaining it almost as much as sailing on it, which he usually did alone. He knew his neighbors, but didn't socialize with them. He wasn't part of the Hamptons social New York crowd. He remained an outsider and a visitor, and was content to do that. Entering the local social whirl would have been a burden and an intrusion he didn't want to deal with. One of the things he loved about the Hamptons was that you could live life there however you wanted, quietly alone, or as part of all the social events that went on constantly. He could be himself there. And Liam enjoyed seeing that side of him, and sharing the rare downtime with his father. Charlie wasn't stressed here, barely checked his emails, just enough to stay in touch with his office. He was fully accessible for emergencies, but he tried not to engage in July and August, and he and Liam had long talks about life as they lay in the sun on the deck, or looked up at the stars at night with a glass of wine. Charlie had always treated him like an adult, which Liam appreciated. They had a relationship of mutual respect.

They'd been there for a week when Liam cautiously told his father that he didn't want to go back to Yale, or at least not yet. While exploring châteaux in France and famous castles in England, Liam had found that he was more fascinated by their gardens and parks and mazes than he was by the actual structures. For him, the gardens were living, breathing beings that grew and changed and evolved and combined historical designs with newer techniques. He had found a French school that taught landscape architecture, and he wanted to defer his graduate studies, to focus on that and study in France for a year. As he put it very modestly, he had discovered that he wanted to be a "gardener" when he grew up. It was a great deal more than that. Le Nôtre, the master designer of the gardens of Versailles, had even laid out parts of Washington, D.C., originally. Liam shared his dreams with his father, and Charlie didn't want to disappoint him, although he wished that Liam had loftier aspirations than working on gardens.

Liam saw the opportunities as limitless, to work on parks, historical châteaux, and more modern outdoor spaces around museums, monuments, and even grand private estates. It could be as simple as a country cottage or something as major as Versailles, with a full range in between. Charlie was reminded of the times when he had tried to share his visions of the future with his father, and he had brutally crushed Charlie's dreams and dismissed them. He didn't want to do the same to Liam, and had to force himself to open his mind, broaden his view, give up his own aspirations for his son, and listen to what he wanted. Liam said he couldn't discuss it with his mother, who only saw two templates for his future: law school or business school. No other options were acceptable to her, as Charlie knew. She had no imagination or tolerance for anything outside those fields, and thought that any other plan spelled disaster. Charlie wanted to respect who Liam was and what he wanted, even if it wasn't what he had envisioned for him. He could still remember his father derisively calling him The Delivery Boy and The Fast Food King when he established his two startups. He was determined not to do the same, when Liam called himself a "simple gardener." His dreams were far more sophisticated than that, and he had a real connection to the earth, the way Charlie did with business in a way his own father had never understood, nor tried to.

When Liam explained his plans to his father, he looked at him with hope in his eyes, and Charlie didn't have the heart to dash it. His real goal for Liam was for him to be happy and fulfilled in his life, and if building magnificent gardens was his passion, who was he to belittle it or say he was wrong?

"I know it must sound crazy to you, Dad, and it's about as far as you can get from what you and Mom do, in the world of finance and venture capital and startups, but it's what I love." He was so simple and direct as he said it, and so humble, that all of Charlie's hesitations dissolved, and he smiled at his son.

"You have to do what you love, Liam. That's where it has to start. I love the businesses I've been in. It's a game I love, starting from nothing except some crazy idea and building something I can turn into a giant if I do it right and get lucky. Like you starting with a seed, and turning it into a garden like Versailles. It's the same principle. And your mother has a real talent for venture capital. You have my blessing if you need it, to do whatever you have to do to get there. Don't ever let anyone stand in the way of your dreams, not even your mom or me.

"You need that passion to have a worthwhile life. Don't ever lose that, or let anyone talk you out of it. Fight for it if you have to. This is your life and no one else's. Don't let anyone spoil it for you, or stop you. That's what my father tried to do. He tried to shame me out of my dreams. I didn't let him, and it cost me his respect and my relationship with him. But I don't regret it even today. I won't ever do that to you. The price is too high, and no one wins. I lost a father and he lost a son that way. I won't let that happen to us. So go for it, if building gardens is your passion and what turns you on. That's a hell of a lot more noble than what I did—I turned delivering condoms and mattresses to my classmates into a major career. What you want to do is beautiful and could last for centuries. How could I say no to that?" Liam looked ecstatic when his father said it, and deeply touched. As independent as he was, his father's approval was important to him, and he knew he wouldn't get it from his mother, who had no artistic or creative interest, and no ability to use her creativity except for money and deals. She was a genius with that, but gardens would be totally beyond her, and Charlie knew it too. Liam wouldn't get the blessing he wanted from her, but what his father had just said to him was enough. Charlie had just given him wings to fly. It was what Charlie had always hoped to get from his father, and never did. He had only gotten his anger, disapproval, and harsh criticism. Liam deserved better than that, and so had Charlie at his age. He had had to fly against his father's wishes and take to the skies alone. And even if earthbound himself, and limited in his knowledge of Liam's chosen field, he wanted to give Liam a good send-off and wish him well.

The two men grew closer than they'd ever been in the time they spent together at the house in East Hampton. The pain in Liam's ankle was easing, and he had gotten adept with the crutches. The only help Charlie provided was hanging out in the bathroom when Liam took a shower to make sure he didn't fall, hopping on one leg with a plastic garbage bag protecting the injured one. Other than that, Liam managed fine, and peaceful nights, sleep, and the sea air did them both good. They cooked lobster together and made sumptuous dinners, and Charlie introduced Liam to some excellent wines. They were two men who loved and respected each other. One couldn't ask more than that from father or son, and they both flourished in the warmth they shared as they bonded.

Liam had spoken to his mother, and was planning to spend a few days with her on his way home. She had a house full of guests in Aspen, all stars of the venture capital world like her. It was all she knew and they were the only kind of people she wanted to be with. It struck Charlie sometimes that in her own way, she was as limited as her banker father had been. They both had a specific relationship to money, and couldn't see any other way of life as acceptable or of interest. It surprised Charlie because she could be very creative with some of her deals and how to make them work, but it extended no further than the boundaries she established, which were rigid and inflexible.

Even the startups Charlie had successfully established were too far outside the traditional box for her. She didn't get it, and she had dismissed Charlie as a suitable partner because of it. He doubted that she would be any more indulgent with their son. He suspected that Faye would override Liam's wishes and insist on law school or business school as she always did. Liam feared it too. He was planning to go forward anyway, but he was hoping for both his parents' approval, out of respect for them. Charlie thought it was more than they deserved, since they had served their own interests for so long. Charlie was determined to honor Liam's wishes, but knowing Faye, he doubted that she would agree. It was her way or the highway. Charlie wanted to apply a lighter hand and had offered his support. He had made the suggestion that Liam defer Yale for a year, rather than withdraw completely, in case he discovered that landscape architecture was less exciting than he thought. He advised him to keep his options open rather than close any doors, which Liam thought was wise, and agreed to do. He was grateful for his father's advice.

Aside from their serious talks, they had fun together. They couldn't pursue the sports they enjoyed, like tennis or biking or long walks on the beach, but they took drives in the area, cooked together, and went out for good meals. They played video games

The Portrait

and Charlie was a grossly incompetent adversary, much to Liam's delight, and Liam told him about some of the girls he had dated recently, none of them serious. They spoke openly on many subjects, which led Liam to venture onto a topic he had always wondered about and they had never discussed. It was an unspoken taboo. It came up one night, as they lay on the deck outside the living room, gazing at the stars.

"What went wrong with you and Mom? How did you end up so far apart?" Liam dared to ask him, and Charlie hesitated before he answered, pondering the reasons himself, while Liam worried he had gone too far and offended him, and had risked their recent closeness with the question.

"I'm not sure there is a simple answer to that," Charlie finally said, glancing at Liam and then back up at the sky. There was a falling star at that exact moment, as there often was in the summer when he was there. He loved watching them as they free-fell through the heavens and disappeared. "My personal opinion is that marriage is a crapshoot at best. Whatever age you marry, twenty, thirty, forty, you don't know who you're going to be a decade later, or who your partner will be, what you'll want, if you'll still want the same things or something completely different. People don't grow in the same way, like plants, I guess. If you're lucky, you grow in the same direction as life bends you. If not, you end up going in opposite directions, and can't even see each other anymore.

"For sure, we were too young. I don't think either of us was thinking about marriage. We were both under a lot of pressure at Harvard, and trying to excel. We were both driven about our studies, and I think your mother went through some kind of rebellious stage. When I met her she was thirty-one, I was five years younger, and maybe turning thirty made her a little crazy for a minute. She had purple hair, and wore the shortest skirts I'd ever seen. She could drink any guy under the table, and still ace her exams the next day, while I had to struggle for good grades. I thought she was the coolest girl I had ever met, and the smartest. I loved how smart she was, and she was fun to be with. We went to Vegas on a lark. I won five thousand dollars playing craps, while she kept explaining the odds to me. She was good at that too. And I don't even remember how we wound up at the Elvis Chapel, but we did. She was holding a bouquet of fake flowers, I was wearing a white rhinestone-studded Elvis cape—and I only remember that because we have a picture of it—and the next morning, I had the worst hangover of my life and a fake gold ring on my finger, and we were really married. We went to an oxygen bar for our hangovers and real life set in. The obvious moral of the story is that you don't marry someone you barely know when you're drunk off your ass. We talked about getting it annulled, and not even telling anyone we'd done it. But we were young and smart, we liked each other and had fun together, and by the time we landed in Boston, we decided to give it a shot, and exit quietly if it didn't work. We said a year. We told our parents, which was a mistake, and they went nuts. We should have kept it to ourselves. It was bumpy while she finished law school and I got my MBA in the next few months. We were both beginning to think it wasn't going to work, but we wanted to give it a fair chance after we graduated, and six months after my moment of glory in the Elvis cape, she found out she was pregnant, and we both decided to take it seriously. There was no way back at that point. Abortion and divorce were out of the question for both of us. So we were stuck, and you were the only sweet spot in the story.

"Her moment of rebellion passed, and she became pretty much who she is now. Driven, serious, conservative, brilliant at her job, passionate about her career, committed to excellence, with a lot of sharp edges. Life with two big careers and a child is serious stuff. Neither of us was ready for kids. We put all our energy into our careers and not our marriage. I'm sorry I didn't spend more time with you. I regret that now. I'm not sure if Faye and I were too much alike or not enough alike. Her work means everything to her, as mine does to me too. She has one speed. I wanted more, and I don't think she had it in her. I can't tell you when it happened. Things like that happen over time, but one day about fifteen years later, we both knew it was over. There was nothing left. We agreed to stay together because we thought a divorce would be a mess. She said it would be "expensive and inconvenient," which is true, but it would have been the healthier choice. We told ourselves we were staying together for you, which sounds noble, but wasn't true. We stayed because we were too lazy and scared to deal with our mistakes and face the unknown. You haven't really been home in eight years, and we're still there, like strangers under one roof, so there isn't even a noble excuse for it anymore. I'm not sure why people stay together in circumstances like ours. Laziness, habit, fear of what's out there, or what isn't. The cost of tearing a life in half, and losing half of it. Maybe it's all about the fear and loss. You forget that other people actually live together and love each other. You put up with not having human warmth and affection for so long that it begins to seem normal, not to have it, but it isn't normal, it's a terrible mistake and it's sad, and a hard way to live."

"I used to wonder," Liam said, "why other people's parents hugged and kissed and liked each other, and you and Mom didn't. You never touched each other, you were hardly around at the same time, and you both looked miserable when you were together. I couldn't understand why you were together. The divorced parents of my friends looked happier. I get it now. Marriage seems scary to me. How hard it must be to get it right, and to still love each other twenty years later."

"You have to put energy and effort into it," Charlie told him, "like watering a garden. We didn't water the garden. We spent no time together. We were damn lucky with how you turned out, with so little time and effort on our part. That's a tribute to you, not to us," Charlie said, and Liam smiled. "And our careers are in great shape. The marriage probably never would have worked, but we didn't do anything to help it. Life just doesn't work that way," he said realistically. "And I think your mom is comfortable the way it is now, with the trappings of marriage, and the appearance of it, without the burdens and responsibilities of a real marriage. We both gave up years ago. I guess that's your answer. It was a long shot. It was a long shot in the beginning, and we gave up."

Liam knew that—he had lived it and seen it firsthand. His friends had envied him the freedoms he had, but he knew he had grown up with two parents who didn't love each other. It was like living in a concrete wasteland where nothing grew. He had spent

The Portrait

all the time he could at his friends' homes, basking in the warmth of their families, since he didn't have his own. It had been enough to keep him going, and his own inner strength had gotten him through, but he didn't want a marriage like his parents' one day. Being alone seemed better to him than a life like theirs. His father had been honest with him, and didn't dress it up, or give Faye and himself purer motives as an excuse.

"Do you think you and Mom would ever get divorced?" Liam asked the question he had wondered all his life. The icy chasm between his parents had existed for as long as he could remember. Not only did they not see each other, they didn't like each other. Charlie hesitated for a moment before he answered.

"I don't know. I think your mom is comfortable the way things are. And I'm used to it too. It takes a lot of guts to take everything apart and start over. And your mother wasn't wrong when she said a divorce would be a huge financial mess." They could afford to get divorced, but Charlie wasn't sure that either of them wanted to. They were used to their life the way it was. It was predictable. There was nothing unknown to fear.

"Maybe you'd both be happier," Liam said gently, with youthful wisdom. His parents weren't old, but they had given up on love, both of them. He knew from what his mother told him that she had had the love and approval of her parents, until she had married Charlie, irresponsibly. Liam knew too that his father had never been loved since his own mother's death. Charlie had forgotten what being loved felt like, or maybe he didn't think he deserved it. But he had the love of his son now, which warmed his heart, even if he thought he didn't deserve that either. Liam wondered if his father had other women in his life, but he didn't ask him. He didn't want to know, and to share a secret like that would be a betrayal of his mother. And he was sure his father wouldn't have told him. He was an honorable man, and hadn't told Liam anything he didn't already know, or had guessed. The lack of love between his parents was so obvious, and had been all his life, whatever the reason for it, or if it had ever existed. It didn't now, which was all that mattered.

They lay there quietly on the deck for a long time after all that Charlie had said. They finished their wine and got up from their chairs to go to bed. Liam was grateful for what his father had told him, and for his honesty. Charlie added one more thing before they went to their rooms. "Your mom is my family. You and she are the only family I have. And the greatest thing she ever gave me was you. I will always be grateful to her for that," he said in a husky voice, and they hugged each other. "Maybe that's enough," he said, and Liam hugged him tight for a moment.

"Thank you, Dad." Liam had tears in his eyes, which Charlie didn't see as they held each other. It had been an important moment between them, of honesty about his parents' lives and how they felt about each other and about him. Liam was grateful for the independence they had given him, which had allowed him to grow up early and find his own direction. He felt sorry for his father, and sad that he was willing to settle for so little warmth in his life, except from his son. That didn't seem like enough to Liam. He could see the price his parents had paid for a loveless marriage, and it seemed like too high a price to him.

For the rest of the time Liam spent with his father in the Hamptons, they had a wonderful time. When he could put a little more weight on his injured leg, they walked around the local towns. They went fishing together. Liam was stopping to see his mother in Aspen on the way home, despite her houseguests, and was going to try to tell her his plans. He had made up his mind. He was going back to France at the end of August, and before that he was going to enroll online in the landscaping school he was excited about. It seemed like it would open so many doors to him, and he loved the idea of working outside. It suited him and it would use his drawing skills, just as traditional architecture would have. He was sure this was the right path for him, and Charlie respected the passion he had for it.

The day before Liam left for Aspen, Charlie took him to the bookshop in East Hampton, and Liam found three big books about gardens. They were a popular category for people in the area, seeking to design the gardens for their estates. Charlie bought the books for him, and Liam was talking about them excitedly as they left the bookshop, like a kid with a new toy he couldn't wait to play with. It made Charlie smile. He knew what it was like to have that kind of enthusiasm and passion for what you wanted to do.

Charlie was listening to Liam tell him about a garden he had seen in England with a maze that was two hundred years old, when he bumped into a woman on her way in at the bottom of the steps. He apologized immediately and looked at her and was suddenly stunned to find himself looking into a familiar pair of green eyes. It was Devon, and he was so startled to see her that he didn't speak for a minute but quickly recovered.

"What a surprise to see you," he said, and introduced her to

Liam, who looked intrigued by her. There was something very gentle and ethereal about her which struck him.

"I spend the summer here, painting whatever I want," she explained. "I have an old barn. It's like camping out and I love it. It renews my energy before I go back to my real work in September," she said, smiling at Charlie, and including Liam in her warmth. "Do you have a house here?" she asked.

"I've been renting the same one every year for ten years. So far, they won't sell it to me, but hope springs eternal. I love it here too."

"I'm surprised I haven't seen you at the bookstore before. They have wonderful art books. I'm their biggest fan."

"Liam is going to be designing gardens. They had some beautiful garden books."

"You'll have to come and visit my barn," she included them both in the invitation.

"Liam is leaving tomorrow, but I'd love to see it," Charlie said warmly, and Liam thought his father looked nervous when he spoke to her, and almost boyish. He had noticed how beautiful she was, in a totally natural way, with her red hair and no makeup, a pink T-shirt and paint-splattered jeans, and sandals. She fit right in to the local scene. Liam guessed her to be about thirty, which was what she looked like.

Charlie promised to call her and they left, while he tried to look less excited to see her than he was.

"Who is she, Dad?" Liam asked as they walked back to the car, with Liam still on his crutches. Charlie tried to look casual about it.

"She's a famous artist. Devon Darcy. She's a portrait painter, and

The Portrait

paints mostly famous people. The bank wants me to have a portrait done for the boardroom. She's going to start a portrait of me in January, if I have time." He tried to sound offhanded as they got into the car.

"Wow, that doesn't sound like you," Liam commented. "Like the one of Granddad?" he asked, and Charlie laughed.

"I hope not. Her style is more contemporary. Her portraits are really beautiful. I went to a gallery show of hers in New York. She does very impressive work."

"She's beautiful," Liam said, as though his father might not have noticed. Charlie's insides had turned to mush again when he saw her, which Liam didn't have any way of knowing, and didn't suspect. Charlie was always so sensible, and wasn't a flirt with women. He was very straightforward and direct, and treated men and women the same.

"Yes, she is," Charlie agreed noncommittally, and they drove back to the house where Liam pored over the books they had bought before putting them in his suitcase.

Charlie was sending him to Aspen on his plane, so he wouldn't have to struggle in an airport with his crutches, and he was sad to see him go.

They had their last lobster dinner together that night, and played a video game, which Charlie lost as usual, much to Liam's delight. They lay on the deck chairs afterward under a starry sky. Liam's stay there had been the best part of the summer, for both of them, in spite of Liam's broken ankle, which had slowly become less painful, and he was becoming more mobile. He was sorry to leave. He and his father had never been closer, with no other distractions around them. He was grateful for all the advice Charlie had given him, and for the explanations about his parents' marriage, which shed some light on the past for him. When he was younger, he had thought that he was a disappointment to them, so they paid little attention to him and often ignored him. He realized now that it had nothing to do with him. They were just intent on pursuing their own lives and ignoring each other. It was a relief to have some acknowledgment of it. He had gotten trapped in the arctic freeze of their unfortunate marriage. He was grateful for his father's honesty about it. He was old enough to understand it now, and felt sorry for him.

Liam left the house at six A.M. to get to Teterboro in time for an early departure on his father's plane. Charlie got up at five to make him breakfast and help him gather up his things, and get organized with his crutches. He carried everything to the car for him, while the driver carried Liam's small bag he had brought from Europe, along with several shopping bags he'd added, with things Charlie had bought him in the Hamptons, including a pair of cowboy boots he loved that he could wear when he got rid of the orthopedic boot.

"I'm going to miss you, Dad," Liam said softly. He'd never said that to him before, and he meant it.

"I'll miss you too. I'll try to get back to San Francisco before you leave, and if you leave before that, I'll come to see you in Paris." Liam smiled when he said it. "And don't let your mom shake you up about your plans. It's a big stretch for her, but she'll get used to

The Portrait

it." Liam was anxious about the conversation he wanted to have with her. "I'll talk her down after you tell her." They had agreed that the announcement of his change of direction should come from Liam, not his father. He was an adult, and he wanted to act like one, but he had no illusions that she would greet the news with delight or even approval. He just had to work his way through it. She could be daunting, and very cold.

"I had a wonderful time," he told his father again, as he stood next to the car, leaning on his crutches. He was tempted to stay but he still wanted some time at home to see his friends before they all left again at the end of the summer. Some of them were starting jobs in other cities, or going on to graduate school, since they had all graduated from college in May and June. A few of them were staying in San Francisco, but not many. The only good jobs available to them were at the tech companies. For those interested in other fields, San Francisco had little to offer so they had to go to other, bigger cities to find jobs.

Charlie hugged him one last time and helped him into the car. Liam opened the window and waved as they headed down the driveway, and Charlie waved until the car turned onto the road. Liam couldn't see it, but there were tears rolling down his father's cheeks. The weeks with him were everything Charlie had hoped to share with him, and more. He was so glad he had gone to Paris to rescue his son and bring him back. It was the beginning of the solid foundation of their relationship as two men who loved and admired each other. Charlie couldn't wish for more, as he walked slowly back into the house and put their breakfast dishes into the dishwasher.

He glanced at the kitchen wall clock. It was six-thirty. After running into Devon the day before, he had promised himself he was going to call her at ten, which seemed a respectable hour to call. She had invited him to come and see her at her barn, and he wanted to do that. He assumed that her cell phone would reach her. It had bowled him over to see her, and he wanted to see her again. He hadn't called her the night before, on Liam's last night. Seeing her made him feel like an awkward boy again, as naïve and inexperienced as his son. It was amazing how you could feel awkward and off balance at any age, no matter how old and experienced you were. Seeing Devon made him feel young again, like starting all the way back at the beginning with a clean slate.

Chapter 5

Charlie went for an early morning run on the beach, to pass the time before he felt he could call Devon. He didn't want to call her too early and wake her, since he didn't know her habits. He came back after running several miles along the beach, took a shower, poured himself a cup of coffee, and reached for his cellphone. He called her on her cell since it was the only number he had, and assumed she would use it in the Hamptons too. He hoped he was right.

The phone rang three times, and then he heard the sensual silk of her voice.

"Devon? It's Charlie Taylor," he began, feeling awkward and nervous, not sure how she would feel about his calling. He was afraid that she would guess his fascination with her. It never occurred to him that she might be equally intrigued and taken with him. She had seemed happy to see him the day before.

"It was nice to see you yesterday. Your son is such a handsome young man." Liam looked just like Charlie, except he was blond like his mother, instead of dark-haired like his father. Other than that they nearly looked like twins. They even had the same height, shape, and broad shoulders.

"Thank you. He's a great kid. He broke his ankle in France, so I rescued him and brought him here," he explained. "He just left a few hours ago. I was happy to run into you too."

"This is my refuge from work. I spend my summers here, in my barn, painting anything I want. There was a deer in my garden yesterday, a doe. She let me photograph her. I'm painting her today. It's a nice change from my serious commissions ten months a year." Charlie realized that the portraits must take intense concentration, getting to know each subject, and trying to learn enough about them to paint them with the depth and insight that she did. It was arduous work, combining discipline, psychology, and art.

He decided to take a bold leap with the next question, and held his breath after he did. "You very generously invited me to come and see you at your barn sometime. I'd love to do that, or have you come to my place for a drink." He tried to sound casual about it, though he was anything but.

"I'd like that very much," Devon said, sounding sincere. "Why don't you come by the barn this afternoon. I was planning to do some gardening, after I work on the painting of the doe this morning. I try to paint a few hours every day."

"I'd love that," he said enthusiastically, making every effort not to sound too excited so she didn't think he was weird or a stalker of some kind. He had been so persistent the first time he met her that she might have gotten that impression, and it was her job to read people well. He actually did feel a little like a stalker, wanting to see her again. It had been less than two months since their last encounter, and the meeting outside the bookshop had been providential.

"Come around four," Devon suggested. Charlie spent the afternoon reading and trying not to obsess about her.

He put on clean white jeans and a blue shirt to see her, and loafers without socks, which was standard Hamptons attire, and stopped at a bakery to buy some cookies and a box of chocolates to bring her as a gift. He didn't want to arrive empty-handed.

She didn't live far from him, he noticed when he put her address into his GPS. He had rented a station wagon for the time he was in East Hampton. He didn't need or want a fancy car in the Hamptons, although there were plenty of them there. He had enough at home in California, and had no desire to show off or make his presence known during his peaceful summer retreat.

There was a pristine white gate at the entrance to Devon's property, a short winding driveway that obscured the house from the road, and her barn came into view a moment later. It was a beautiful old Victorian barn with white-painted gingerbread trim. It looked like a barn in a fairy tale, like "Hansel and Gretel." The barn was painted a pale dove gray, and there were neat flowerbeds of big white hydrangeas she had planted herself. The land around it looked neat and well maintained. Charlie could sense that it was a place she loved. The driveway was gravel and she came out of the barn as soon as she heard him arrive. She was wearing cutoff denim shorts with a pink shirt, her red hair piled on top of her head, to keep it out of her way, and she smiled as soon as she saw him. She looked happy to see him, which warmed his heart. She looked young and fresh and casual, in sandals she had bought in Italy that laced up her legs. She still had a European look to her, as he handed her the cookies and chocolates, and she thanked him warmly. He noticed that she was wearing no makeup. She didn't need it. Her all-seeing green eyes were enough.

She invited him into the barn, which seemed enormous once he walked inside. It was all one space but she had divided it into a sleeping area, with a big four-poster bed draped in mosquito netting, and an inviting sitting area with a comfortable couch and chairs around a coffee table made of an antique door. There was a modern-looking open kitchen, and most of the space was a studio with several easels, canvases leaning against the walls, and her paintings all over the walls. Paintings of animals and children and dogs, still lifes of flowers, and portraits of people. Her distinctive style was visible in each of them, but the subjects were atypical for her, which was what she loved about doing them—a lamp, a goat, a cocker spaniel with a woeful expression, a child on a swing, a lobster, a brightly colored bird, and the painting of the doe on the easel in its earliest stages. Each painting was done in her remarkable technique, with infinite precision and expertise, with the soul of the subject leaping from the canvas. She had an incredible talent, which he already knew.

"This is my happy place," she said with a smile, as she set the cookies and chocolates down in the kitchen. "I love it here." She beamed at him as she said it, and exuded an aura of pure joy. She looked much happier than she had in the city, but there he had

The Portrait

caught her on a workday, in the midst of a commission, and wanting one himself. Here, he wanted nothing from her, and she didn't have to please anyone but herself. She painted the subjects she wanted to, and had fun with them. Some of the paintings were more playful than the subjects he'd seen at her show. But he would have fallen in love with these too. She was an incomparable artist, and her training and technique were flawless on each canvas he saw.

"I love the paintings you do here," he said, looking at them with pleasure. They made him happy too. He studied the beginnings of the doe. It had a graceful elegance to it, with green leafy trees all around.

"I was really angry at her." Devon laughed about the doe. "She ate two of my flowerbeds and trampled a third, but she was so beautiful I couldn't stay mad at her. I got some great photos of her before she ran away. She leaped over my back fence, and now I'm painting her. The dog belongs to my neighbor," she said as he studied the cocker spaniel. "The paintings I do here are just for fun. Sometimes I give them away." He thought the recipients would be very lucky, as he would be when he sat for a portrait by her. But what she did here had a sense of freedom to it. Looking at her paintings was like listening to music—it had a magic and a melody all its own.

She offered him a choice of iced tea or lemonade, and he declined both. They sat down in the sitting area, which was comfortable and easy, with the antique door that served as a coffee table.

"I made the table myself. I found the door at the dump. I find treasures there sometimes," she said, looking relaxed as she smiled at him. "I made the dining table too." It sat in the kitchen area, and could seat eight people. "I don't entertain here, so it's really just for me. My apartment in the city has to look respectable since I paint my subjects there. But I can do whatever I want here, without worrying about what it looks like." It was extremely neat and well curated. She had beautiful taste, with delicate vases on tables, others filled with flowers. The fabrics on her furniture were beautiful. And she had several antique French rugs in the various areas. She had kept the original wooden barn floor, which had charm too. Charlie loved being there with her.

They chatted for an hour about nothing in particular. He didn't want to overstay. He was sure she had things to do, and the painting she was working on, if nothing else. He got up to go, and she walked him back outside to his car. There was a rabbit poised near it, and it ran away as they approached.

"Another subject?" he teased her.

"I think the first year I was here, I must have painted thirty of them. I've sworn off rabbits. I can't keep up with them. I have a weakness for lambs and goats. They have so much charm," she said, and he smiled. She had a light touch that he liked, although he could sense that she had a very serious side. He liked the combination of both.

"Could I take you to dinner tomorrow night?" he asked her cautiously, not sure how she'd respond, and afraid of a rejection. He wasn't sure how to approach her, and didn't want to blow it. She smiled up at him when he asked her.

"That would be very nice," she said. "I don't go out very often

The Portrait

when I'm here." He was pleased that she'd accepted, and smiled at her.

"Is there anywhere special you'd like to go?" he asked her.

"Someplace simple where we can talk. I don't like noisy restaurants, or very fancy ones," she said shyly.

"Neither do I. You have to come and see my place sometime. It's right on the beach. I love going for long walks, and seeing the ocean. I have an old-fashioned widow's walk. I can spend hours watching the sea."

"I love the ocean too," she said, as he got in his car.

"Shall I pick you up at seven-thirty?" She nodded with a smile and looked like a young girl. It felt like an old-fashioned courtship, which had never happened to him before. He was a married man, and most of the women he'd gone out with while he was married were bold, independent, and well aware of his status, and it was an even exchange of sexual favors. It didn't have the cautious innocence of his conversations with Devon, or the respect he felt for her.

He realized then that she didn't know he was married, and he wanted to tell her in some nonthreatening way. She wouldn't be a homewrecker for having dinner with him. There was no home to "wreck" in his case, or a loving wife at home for him to cheat on. They were two somewhat jaded long-term strangers living at the same address, with no illusions about a relationship that had died years before. He didn't want Devon to feel guilty for going out with him, if they saw each other again, and he hoped they would. She was a lovely person, and a hugely talented artist, with a big reputation of her own. She didn't need him for fame and fortune. It was a strictly human encounter between two people who were alone and admired each other. The possibilities were both endless and limited. He couldn't offer her a future, but he could offer her a very agreeable present, if it ever came to that, as long as they understood each other and she knew what the ground rules were. Or she might have no interest in knowing him better. He couldn't read her yet, didn't know her well enough to sense if she was open to anything with him, other than a commission for a portrait. But he loved getting acquainted with her, and seeing her in her barn, which was her natural habitat and summer residence. He wanted to walk on the beach with her, and spend time with her. He wondered if she liked to sail. There was so much that was a mystery to him and he wanted to learn, if she was open to it. Discovering more about her excited him too.

Charlie drove back to his house, happy to have seen her, and looking forward to the following night. He reserved a table at a lovely restaurant with outdoor dining on a beautiful terrace. It was one of the nicer restaurants in East Hampton, but wasn't overly fancy, and it was quiet, just as she said she liked. He hadn't had dinner there yet this summer, because Liam was more of a burger-and-fries kind of guy, and they both loved lobster dinners. Devon seemed more delicate and refined.

He could hardly wait to have dinner with her. When he went to pick her up the next day, it felt like a date, and he wasn't sure if it was. Whatever it was or turned out to be, he was enjoying every minute of it.

Devon came out of the barn to greet him, wearing a flowing

The Portrait

white gauzy skirt, a matching white blouse with big bell sleeves, and silver sandals. She looked summery and feminine. They drove to the restaurant, and she loved it when she saw it, and thanked him. The food was French and delicious. They talked about Europe and her studies at the Beaux-Arts, he explained his startups to her, and the conversation flowed. They were the last people in the restaurant and it had been a wonderful evening for both of them. They left the restaurant still talking, and Charlie made her laugh at his descriptions of his first startup, while he was at Princeton, and the crazy things he had delivered. Devon spoke sparingly of certain periods of her early life, although she talked about her studies and her grandmother. She had said she was a widow but hadn't explained the circumstances of her husband's death, and he didn't pry. He could sense that there were things she didn't talk about, that were probably painful for her, and he didn't want to know what she didn't want to tell. They were comfortable together and he didn't want to spoil that. Devon was like a beautiful animal in the wild that had to be approached at its own pace. He didn't want to rush her or frighten her. He could sense that parts of her were fragile, and he respected that.

When they got home to the barn, she didn't invite him in, which could have been awkward since her bedroom was part of the entire open space. He stopped at the door, and she thanked him for the evening, with a look in her eyes that reached deep inside him and grabbed his heart. Unable to stop himself, Charlie leaned down and kissed her gently on the lips, and she didn't resist him. She melted into his arms, and they were both breathless when they stopped kissing. He could feel a passion in her that he hadn't suspected before. She concealed it well. They kissed again, and she finally gently pulled away, smiled mysteriously, and floated into the barn with a wave as she closed the door. He drove away a minute later, feeling his emotions doing somersaults in his chest. Devon was as magnetic and mesmerizing as she had been since the first moment he'd seen her. He could hardly keep his head on straight. It had been a perfect evening, and he fell asleep that night dreaming of her.

She sent him a text the next day, thanking him for a wonderful evening. She sounded so warm and friendly that it made him brave enough to invite her to his place for a drink, the next day, and he offered to make dinner for her if she liked lobster or pasta, which he said were the only two things he knew how to cook.

She texted back "Pasta, thank you." And he responded, "Six o'clock and a walk on the beach before dinner?" And the answer came back, "Perfect. See you at six tomorrow." It was a simple, friendly, efficient exchange.

He bought the groceries the next day to make pasta carbonara, which he had learned to make the authentic way in Italy. He was wearing jeans and a white shirt when she arrived promptly at six in a red T-shirt and jeans and red satin ballet flats. She looked casual and sexy. He had set the table with the owners' placemats and china, all of which were informal. He tried to make it all look friendly and not like a seduction scene, which would have been premature. He wanted to show her his surroundings, and make her feel at ease there with him.

She loved the house when he showed her around, and the weather cooperated perfectly. There was a light breeze when they

The Portrait

left their shoes at the house and headed to the beach. It was gorgeous, and there were children playing and dogs running, women talking and couples kissing, as Devon picked up the occasional seashell and carried it with her. She rolled up her jeans and waded in the surf. She had worn her hair down and it flew around her in the breeze. They walked for an hour and went back to the house. He prepared the carbonara, and a salad, and the pasta was delicious.

They talked nonstop and there was always more to say. They never tired of talking to each other. It struck him at one point that he had talked more to Devon in two days than he had to Faye in the last two years. It was the hallmark of their crazy situation. He and Faye had run out of things to say to each other twenty years before, but they were still married. He wanted to explain it as simply as he could to Devon when they finished dinner. He didn't want to keep it from her any longer. She needed to know his circumstances, whatever happened, even as a friend.

"I want to explain something to you, in the interest of full disclosure," he said, as he set down a bowl of lemon and chocolate gelato in front of her, with chocolate-covered biscotti. It had been a real Italian meal, and she loved it. He looked serious when he sat down across from her, and she waited to hear what he said. She could sense that it was important.

"I didn't say anything to you before, because my circumstances are somewhat strange, and don't make a lot of sense to most people, or even to me sometimes. I'm married, but not in the classic sense. We got married on the spur of the moment in grad school, on a crazy weekend in Las Vegas, it was a mistake, we didn't know each other well. We were planning to dissolve it and discovered that my son was on the way, so we stuck with it, and compounded the mistake. The situation deteriorated over the years, and basically, the marriage died a long time ago. It was never really a functioning marriage. About a dozen years ago, we knew it was over, and ten years ago we gave up on it completely. We had a child and thought we should stay together for his sake, which was probably also a mistake. And as my wife said so succinctly, a divorce would be inconvenient, unpleasant, and expensive, so we agreed not to get divorced but to live our own lives, separately but in the same house 'for our son,' which is what we've done. It has its advantages and disadvantages, and it balances out. We are equally disengaged. We are married in name only, living at the same address. And admittedly cutting everything in half now would be a mess financially. We have very little contact with each other. We go our own ways. Liam has left home, so we can't even dignify our relationship by claiming it's for him anymore. Call it laziness or cowardice or habit, we're still technically married, although I probably have less contact with her than I do with my mailman. There are no jealous scenes, no vacations together. We live separately in the same home, but we're strangers to each other. I've been involved with other women over the years, no one I was in love with. I've never made anyone any promises, nor broken any. I have no idea what she does, and it's none of my business. I feel totally comfortable going anywhere with you. I have nothing to hide, but I thought it's fair for you to know that legally, for financial reasons if nothing else, I'm married, although my heart isn't involved and neither is hers. I see no advantage in

The Portrait

changing that. I'm not a prospect for anyone's future, but my heart is free, my time is my own, and I owe no one any explanations. I'm a free man, but not legally, and I thought you should know." The situation sounded even stranger when he had to explain it to someone. He hadn't in a long time, but he was taken enough with Devon that he wanted her to know and didn't want to mislead her. She looked at him seriously when he had finished.

"That's so sad. It sounds so lonely," she said, gently touching his hand. She didn't look upset, she was sorry for him, and he was startled by her reaction, which was one of compassion, not disappointment or anger that he hadn't told her sooner.

"As an example," he added, "she vacations in Aspen, I come here, and we won't speak to each other all summer. We have no reason to. We pass each other in the halls occasionally when I'm home. I travel a lot. We have nothing to say to each other. There's nothing left to say. Staying married in those conditions must sound crazy to you, and it does to me too, but she's my family in a way, and I have no desire to cut everything I have in half and make our lives less comfortable and more complicated. We waited too long to divide things up, to put it bluntly. It's easier the way it is now than to tear everything apart and start again."

"Did you ever love her?" Devon asked him, getting to the heart of the matter.

"I don't think so. And she didn't love me either. We got married during a drunken weekend in Vegas when we were students. And she changed radically when she grew up. We have nothing in common, except our son." Devon nodded her understanding. She didn't look shocked, which surprised Charlie. He had guessed her to be more traditional than that, but he was grateful and relieved that she hadn't run screaming from the room in horror.

"I was married too," she said quietly. "I was twenty-two when we married, he was twenty-four, we were students at the Beaux-Arts. He eventually gave up his studies so he could support me. He was such a sweet boy. We were children. And he was so good to me. Four years later, he was hit by a bus riding his bike to work on a rainy night, and he was killed. I was a widow at twenty-six. That was sixteen years ago, and I've never wanted to marry since. For a long time, I still felt married to him. I don't anymore. And who knows how it would have been when we grew up. I think it would have worked, we were happy, but you never know. What works at twenty-two doesn't always work at forty-two or fifty-two. We never had a chance to find out. There's never been anyone serious in my life since then. I've focused on my work, and it's been enough for me. Something happened when I saw you for the first time at the gallery. I felt something very strong the moment I saw you, a current between us. I thought that if we were meant to know each other, you would find me. And you did, the next day. Now we've found each other again. I don't know what that means. But I love being with you and talking to you. Thank you for being honest with me," she said gratefully, and he felt a huge weight drop from his shoulders. She was fine with the fact that he was married. And the rest remained to be seen. No one could predict what would happen, but he wanted her to know that marriage wasn't an option, and she seemed fine with it.

"I move around a lot, and I'm used to coming and going as I

need to. I'm very independent, and I'm not used to answering to anyone, I never have been. But I always find my way home eventually." She thought about what he had said, and it sounded reasonable. "Thank you for trusting what I told you. It's not one of those bogus arrangements cheaters claim to have and then their jealous wives go nuts. I have no jealous wife. She couldn't care less what I do, or if I never show up again. In fact, I think it annoys her more than anything when I do come home."

"What does your son think about it?" she asked, curious. "It can't have been easy for him."

"No, it wasn't. Our priority was our careers, which was wrong. He and I just spoke about it. He's very forgiving, which is more than we deserve. He thinks our marriage is a sad way to live, as you just said. But it's how things ended up, very quickly, and it's too complicated to unravel now. Liam basically grew up in a loveless home. He paid the price for our mistake, but he seems to have survived it remarkably well, no thanks to us. He's a strong guy. Maybe he knew that despite our mistakes, we loved him—we just didn't love each other."

"That's not a healthy way to live either, for any of you. And she doesn't want anything better than that?" It was hard to believe, but she trusted what he said.

"All she wants is her career. And she's brilliant at it. It's her first priority, and always was. It was mine too, for a long time, but I want something more in my life now, to the degree that I can have it, in my circumstances. I've been careful not to get involved with people who wanted more from me. I didn't want to let anyone down, break any promises or anyone's heart, and I haven't. But the same rules still apply. I'm limited by my circumstances and what I can give in the context of how I live my life."

"You can give your heart. That's what matters most, Charlie. It's all that matters. Without that, you have nothing, just as you say about your marriage. That's not a life for either of you." She wondered if his wife had a lover and he didn't know.

"No, it's not," he agreed with her, and leaned over and kissed her. They had said enough. She knew what she needed to know. It was a level playing field, as much as he could give her one, and she put her arms around him and kissed him with unbridled passion.

"We found each other for a reason," she whispered to him afterward, "whatever that reason is." He had never known a woman who was as understanding and forgiving and demanded so little from him.

They sat on the deck after dinner, holding hands and talking softly, late into the night. He wanted her to stay, but didn't want to ask her. They had covered some important ground that night, serious things had been said. He didn't want to confuse her. She had told him everything he needed to know, and he had been honest with her. The rest would unfold as it was meant to, and they both knew what they were getting into, if they did. The ground rules were clear. He was falling in love with her, and she with him. It had happened like lightning the first time they saw each other. And the rest of the story wasn't written yet.

Chapter 6

Charlie and Devon had given each other much to think about. She mulled over what he had said the next day while she was painting, and he thought about her all day. His description of his marriage sounded tragic to her, a waste of two lives that had surely impacted their son as well, even if Liam said he had forgiven them, but what a terrible way to live, for all three of them.

She and Jean-Louis had been so loving to each other, and he had been so kind and generous to her, and they had adored their baby Axel when he was born, and after. Jean-Louis had lived for them, and it had nearly killed her when Axel died. Devon couldn't imagine a woman like Faye, or how she and Charlie had continued a loveless travesty of marriage for twenty-three years. And keeping their finances intact seemed like a poor excuse to maintain the marriage. But she respected what he had told her. He had made it clear that he intended to stay married, although he claimed it didn't interfere with his independent life at all and for all intents and purposes he was a free man. It hadn't deterred Devon. She appreciated his honesty, and she was just as attracted to him as before.

Charlie walked around in a daze all day, relieved that she wasn't upset that he was married, although he was sure that she would have preferred it if that wasn't the case. She was the first truly available woman he had ever been attracted to, and he was relieved to know that she wasn't merely an illusion, or an obsession—she was real. It opened the door wide for him to pursue her, and he could hardly stay away from her all day. He couldn't resist calling her at five o'clock. He had thought of nothing else all day. She had looked so beautiful as they talked in the candlelight the night before, with her hair glowing copper in the light, and her eyes bright, filled with trust and hope. She was the most loving woman he had ever met, and the most compelling. All he wanted was to be with her.

"Can I interest you in a walk on the beach?" He liked walking early in the morning or at sundown, when it wasn't as hot and there was usually a breeze.

"I'd love to, maybe tomorrow. I'm just finishing a painting, and I don't want to leave it right now. Do you want to come over in a while?"

"I'd love that," he said in a husky voice, which gave her a thrill. She wanted to see him too, but she was in an awkward place on the painting she was working on.

"Seven o'clock?" she suggested, squinting at the painting. "I could try to cook dinner for us, but you might never want to see me again," she said, and he laughed.

The Portrait

"I can bring pasta and cook for you. My repertoire isn't too varied either, or we can go out." He wanted to see her, he didn't care when or how. He didn't want to waste a minute. All the barriers had been removed, in his eyes, with his disclosure the night before. And she had accepted the situation he was in. Other women had walked out as soon as he said he was married, whatever his arrangement was with his wife. And some just wanted to have fun, or were married too. He had always said that his being married was a given, and a number of women were willing to play by his rules. It meant that they had no future with him, which they accepted for a while, and when they found that it was true, they left. Devon didn't have her eye on the future, she was only living in the present. She had long since learned how unreliable the future was, no matter what plans one made.

Charlie arrived at seven, in jeans and a black T-shirt, after his walk on the beach. And Devon was still wearing the shorts and pink tank top she'd been wearing while painting all afternoon. She had just finished a small painting of a brightly colored bird that had caught her eye that morning. It was like a beautiful little jewel. It was still sitting on her easel to dry, and she was cleaning her brushes when he arrived. And she had a splash of peacock blue paint in her hair. The painting of the deer was on another easel, finished and drying.

She looked so beautiful and natural and innocent when he walked into the room, with the last rays of sun pouring over her hair like molten gold, that she took his breath away, and he walked across the room and kissed her so hard and so long that she couldn't breathe when he stopped.

"I missed you today," he said in the same husky voice she had heard earlier. His obsession with her had gotten the better of him all afternoon, and he could think of nothing else. Without stopping to ask her, he slowly peeled off her tank top, and held her breasts in his hands and bent to kiss them. She didn't stop him, and reached down and unbuttoned his jeans. The brushes she'd been cleaning fell to the floor, as she and Charlie devoured each other like two starving people. Twenty-three years of a life without love overwhelmed him, and sixteen years of her own loneliness turned into a tidal wave of desire, as he carried her to her bed not far from where they stood. Their clothes vanished instantly, and their bodies took over, begging for each other and crying out for love. They fit together like two pieces of a puzzle, and were driven to heights neither of them could remember. It was dark in the room when their lovemaking ended, and they lay next to each other, trying to catch their breath. Charlie looked at her and smiled.

"I'm sorry, Devon . . . I went crazy thinking about you all day."

"Me too," she whispered with a small smile, running her hand lightly over his body again. They had been swept away by their passion, with no regrets. She propped herself up on one elbow, lying on her side as she looked at him seriously. "I've never made love with a married man before," she said thoughtfully. "It didn't seem right." And she knew that technically, it still wasn't now. But after everything he had said, she didn't feel guilty. He had said he was a free man, and she believed him. She had given herself to him heart and soul.

"I'm not married in that way," Charlie reminded her. "And it was

The Portrait

never like this." For an instant, he felt as though Devon owned him now, and the thought of it terrified him and excited him all at the same time, and he wanted her again.

They made love until they couldn't anymore. They ended up in the shower, with the hot water pelting down on them. She looked up at him adoringly, and he thought he had never loved any woman more. He had never known anyone like her, so full of talent and kindness, passion and tenderness.

"I never want to leave you again," he whispered to her. He knew it was too soon to say it, but it was how he felt. They both had years of pent-up emotions and unfulfilled dreams and longing to bring to each other. "Are you hungry?" he asked as they got out of the shower and he admired her perfect body, as she admired his. They had come far in a short time.

"I'm too happy to be hungry." She smiled at him. "Are you?"

"Starving," he admitted. "I know an all-night diner in Bridgehampton. Do you want to go?" he asked, and she laughed. She was pleasantly exhausted but willing to go anywhere with him. They dressed and locked up the barn, and twenty minutes later they were on the way to Bridgehampton. The diner was like something out of a time warp, and there were lots of young people there, and some truck drivers off the main road. Charlie ordered a steak, and she had waffles that were delicious, and when they finished, they went back to the barn.

They took off their clothes and climbed into her big comfortable bed. They were too tired to make love again. It had been a perfect night, and she smiled thinking that it was the first time in years she had spent the night with a man. The moonlight was shining through the tall windows in the barn, and Charlie whispered to her. She was already half asleep.

"I have to leave early tomorrow. I have a meeting."

"Uh-huh," she mumbled and drifted off to sleep, as he looked down at her with love in his eyes, and then fitted his body around her, and fell asleep himself.

When Devon woke in the morning, Charlie was gone. She vaguely remembered his saying something about a meeting but she couldn't remember what. He had left her a note that said only, "I'll call you . . . thank you for the happiest night of my life . . . love, C." It had been the happiest of hers in a long time too. She thought about him as she drank a cup of coffee. He was starving for love in so many ways. She had been alone and lonely for such a long time, and she had lost so many people she loved. Now Charlie had appeared, like an answer to a prayer. She hadn't even been praying for a man in her life. She accepted it as it was. She didn't want more than she had. She thought love was behind her, in the past, and now here he was, exploding with passion and love. It changed everything. She wondered what they would do when he went back to California at the end of August. He said he traveled all the time, so hopefully they would work it out. And she had four commissions to do between September and the end of the year, so she had her commitments too.

She assumed she would hear from Charlie by the end of the day, for a walk on the beach, or dinner, or another night of passion. She was surprised he didn't send her a text, but assumed he was busy, and she didn't know if the meeting was in the city or remote. She didn't remember what he'd said. And she didn't want to disturb him. She played around with a painting she had started and hadn't finished, but lost interest in it after half an hour, thinking about him, and eager to see him again.

By the end of the day, she hadn't heard from him, and was worried. She wondered if something had gone wrong at the meeting. At ten o'clock that night she called him, and it went to voicemail. She just said she was thinking about him, and hung up. He had said he would call her, so it seemed strange he didn't. She finally fell asleep, sure she'd hear from him in the morning. Something might have happened to him. He could have had an accident on the road. She forced herself not to think of anything dramatic in the morning. He had only left her bed twenty-four hours before, and he had only been out of touch for a day. She wasn't going to make a big deal of it when he called. He had only just walked into her life. She couldn't be needy and unreasonable. She was a grown woman and had been alone for sixteen years. She could survive a day or two without him. She didn't own him and he had heavy responsibilities, she reminded herself. A crisis could have come up at the meeting that he was dealing with. But how long did it take to write a text? There were two voices in her head, Reason and Panic, and she was trying to walk a tightrope between the two.

By the end of the day, she still hadn't heard from him and sent him a text that said only, "Are you okay?" There was no immediate answer and none by the next morning. By then, she was sure that something was wrong. But she had no one to call to ask. He hadn't answered her phone message or her text. And he wasn't the kind of man to make love to her and disappear for three days. He was attentive and kind. She felt ridiculous calling hospitals to look for him. She wasn't going to just show up at his house. There might be people there, still in a meeting.

By the end of the third day, she was in despair, and there was a familiar knot in her stomach she hadn't felt in years. She had felt that knot the night Jean-Louis didn't come home from work. He was gone all night and she was livid, thinking he was having an affair. They had had an argument that morning over something stupid, and it didn't warrant staying out all night. She had thought of going to the restaurant where he worked, but didn't want to make a scene.

It had taken the police a full twenty-four hours to come to her apartment and tell her Jean-Louis had died.

All the same familiar feelings washed over her now, and she forced them from her mind. She had to force herself to know that if Charlie hadn't contacted her for three days, there was a reason for it. He was a sensible, responsible man, and he was crazy about her.

She went for a walk on the fourth day to try to stay calm, and that night, anger finally set in. Maybe he was one of those lunatics who convinced you that they were madly in love with you, got you to sleep with them, and then you never heard from them again. It had happened to her once when she was much younger. She had fallen for it, out of loneliness and despair at the time, two years after Jean-Louis died, before Axel got sick, and the guy had just vanished, and called her three months later for a booty call. She

The Portrait

had hung up on him. But Charlie wasn't like that. He couldn't be. He was an adult, and a responsible caring man.

On the fifth day, she was livid, with herself. She had been an idiot, and had been played for a fool. His whole sad story about his wife. He was probably just a chronic cheater and had used her like a hooker or a sex toy. She was mortally embarrassed by how gullible she had been. She realized that she didn't know him at all, and anything was possible. It was all a fantasy, and a bad joke.

She was morbidly depressed when she got up on the sixth day of his silence. There was no explanation by now except that he was a bad guy, and whatever arrangement he had with his wife, she didn't care. She sent him an ice-cold text that he didn't respond to, which was no surprise by now. The only valid excuse for his silence by then was if he had been kidnapped or was dead, neither of which seemed likely. As well-known as he was, his death would have made the front page. She had looked for it, just in case, but the other scenarios she'd imagined were more likely. She had just been a convenient piece of ass and he'd played a game, and she'd fallen for it like the innocent she was. She blamed herself for being gullible and stupid.

She forced herself to get up and go for a long walk on the beach. It was raining and she didn't care. The gray weather suited her mood. She was sorry she had ever let him into her life. She felt foolish and used. And worse than that it had opened old wounds that she thought were long since healed. Her parents, Jean-Louis, Axel, her grandmother. She had lost everyone she loved, through no fault of theirs or her own. They had all died in terrible accidental circumstances, but her heart had read them as abandonments. It had been her nemesis for years, the fear of being abandoned, that it could happen to her again if she loved someone, that she would lose them too. She had only known Charlie for two months, and not consistently—this time for less than two weeks. She had slept with him, which seemed foolish to her now. But the wound he had slashed wide open again had taken years to heal, and he had woken the demons that had tormented her before. The demons of abandonment, when you knew you were alone in the world.

Charlie had reminded her of that fact in spades. She was sure he wasn't dead in a police morgue somewhere, or unidentified in a hospital, as she had feared at first. He had slept with her, played a game of pretend, and walked out on her as though she were of no consequence whatsoever, and not a word of what he'd said had been true, of how extraordinary she was and how much she meant to him. He had used it as a ploy to get her into bed, and it had worked, which was humiliating. She just had to pull herself up out of the hole again. She was the only one there to do it, and she had to depend on herself and no one else. Charlie had played a game with her. So be it. Now the repair work was up to her.

On the seventh day of his disappearance, she scrubbed her house from top to bottom, reorganized her paints, and inventoried her art supplies to order new ones on Monday to replace what she'd used. She was exhausted by the end of the day, and reminded herself of what a therapist had told her, that she could survive the losses, and she was strong enough to do it. There were mean, evil people in the world and she had just come across one of them. It

The Portrait

was bad luck but it wasn't going to kill her. He hadn't raped her or injured her. He hadn't burned her house down or stolen money from her. He was a different kind of thief, who stole hearts and broke them, and preyed on innocents. But she knew better now, and she had the strength she needed to push him out of her head. The wound he had reopened would heal faster this time than her many losses, which had taken years to heal. This was a short unpleasant experience, and she had learned a lesson from it, not to trust charming strangers with her heart.

She had a shot of brandy to calm her nerves before she went to bed, an old recipe of her grandmother's, and was just falling asleep when her cell phone rang. She had forgotten to put it on silent, after her seven-day vigil waiting to hear from him. She reached for the phone and answered it without checking who it was, and heard a deep, husky familiar voice she hadn't heard in a week, and no longer wanted to hear.

"Devon," he said cautiously, as she came fully awake and realized who it was.

"Don't ever call me again," she said, hung up and turned off the phone. She lay awake for a long time after that, unable to sleep, telling herself she had done the right thing. He didn't deserve an audience for some lame explanation that was all lies. There was no possible explanation for having cut her off for a week, and refusing to respond to her or even send her a text to reassure her. She tossed and turned and finally fell asleep. As far as she was concerned, Charles Taylor was dead. She was going to tell the gallery to return his deposit to him. She had no intention of doing a portrait of him, or anything else. She glanced at her phone and saw the silenced messages stacking up. She didn't read them. She wanted nothing to do with him. He had had the use of her body for a night, and had made a fool of her. But the game was over. He didn't get to come back now and do it again.

She woke up in the morning, feeling slightly hung over from the brandy and the lack of sleep, and seven days of anguish before that. She made herself a cup of coffee, made sure the barn door was locked, and hoped he didn't show up. She couldn't stop herself from reading his messages. There were eleven of them, begging her to let him explain. She wouldn't give him the satisfaction and erased them all without responding. She tried to work on a painting, and couldn't, and went for a run on the beach, far away from where his house was. She wanted to clear her mind and she didn't want to run into him. He had humiliated her enough, and genuinely hurt her.

He called her six more times, and sent seven texts. She stopped reading them, and didn't answer his calls. His calls made her feel anxious, but she tried to ignore them. He called her six more times that night, and left messages, begging her to just speak to him once and after that he'd leave her alone. She thought about it, and wondered if she was being cowardly. She hadn't done anything wrong, he had. When he called while she was drinking her morning coffee, she answered, and braced herself for whatever he was going to say.

"Stop calling me," she said for openers. "You had no problem

The Portrait

ignoring me all last week. Pretend it's last week. I don't want to hear anything you have to say. Leave me alone."

"Devon, I understand. Truly, I'm sorry. I ended up with a crisis at the meeting last week, it went on for fourteen hours, and I was exhausted afterward. I was going to call you. I flew to California the next day, and was in meetings all week. By the time I got out, it was too late to call you every night."

"That's terrific, but unless they cut off your fingers, you could have sent me a text. Five words would have done it. 'I'm okay. I love you.' Or two words, 'I'm OK.' That's four letters. I thought you were dead for half the week. After that, I knew I was. You screw me blind like a booty call, and then you walk out of here, and I never hear from you again? What kind of shitty thing is that to do to someone? Don't call me now and tell me you want to see me. I don't want to see you ever again."

"I'm sorry. I really am. I do that. I get single-focused and concentrate on what I'm doing to the exclusion of everything else. I'm not good at communicating. Or at answering to anyone. And we're new. I didn't realize you'd be this upset. I'm flying back from California tonight and I want to see you."

"I don't want to see you. Wouldn't you be upset if I did that to you? Just vanished and didn't answer anything? And how's your noncommunication working out for you?" She could see why his wife hated him, if he did that to her. "And besides, you're married. I've never slept with married men before, and I think I'll stick to that plan. Married men are supposed to treat you better because they feel guilty, not treat you worse because they don't give a damn about you or their wife. Sell that to someone else. Or do it to her."

"I did, for twenty-three years," he said, sounding morose and sorry for himself.

"That's none of my business. It's yours," she said harshly. "Charlie, what you see took me years to glue back together. Everyone I ever loved died. They abandoned me by dying. It wasn't their fault, but they left me here alone to deal with my life by myself, and I have. I created something I can live with. I can't afford someone like you, playing games with me, shutting me out for no reason because you're 'not good at communicating' or you don't tell people where you are, or you want to prove how independent you are. You can prove that to someone else. I can't take a chance on someone like you. The price is too high, just to prove to you and myself that I can survive it. I can't. I know that about myself. So be nice, go away, and try this routine on someone else. Thank you for calling me. I'm glad you're alive. It makes for a nice change, and I hope you work your crisis out. Now you don't need to worry about calling me back or answering my texts. Have a nice life," she said, and ended the call. He called back and she didn't answer. Two hours later, three dozen red roses arrived at her front door from a florist, with a card from Charlie that said, "Please give me another chance. I really do love you." She threw the card away, and left the roses in her garden. She didn't want to see them in the house. She hoped the deer would eat them, and stay away from her flowerbeds.

She was just as upset as she had been when he was stonewalling her the week before and not responding to her messages or

The Portrait

texts. Either he was as big a bastard as she had thought him, or a bigger mess than she had imagined. He seemed so whole and sane and sensible, but he wasn't. Whatever his reasons, his behavior wasn't acceptable and it upset her too much to stay involved with him. She couldn't let him destroy her, and he could, if she let him in, and he did it again. She didn't want to play.

He left her alone for a few hours then, and she didn't thank him for the roses. They were blood money, as far as she was concerned. He had put her through seven days of hell because he was busy. She didn't even know he'd gone back to California. A relationship with him didn't look like a bright loving future to her. And the roses didn't make up for the pain he'd caused her. She was sure he would do it again if this was his standard M.O. She didn't want to try again, no matter how handsome and sexy he was and how appealing. What he had done for the past week didn't appeal to her at all.

She went for a run on the beach that afternoon, and when she came back, there was another text from him, begging her to have dinner with him the next day, or go for a walk on the beach with him to talk things out. She didn't answer, and turned off her phone. She didn't want to give him another chance to hurt her again. She didn't want to go through another week like the one she'd just been through.

Chapter 7

Charlie saw Liam in the kitchen, the morning he was flying back to the Hamptons. Liam looked serious, and was happy to see his dad. He had gotten back from Aspen a few days before.

"How did it go with your mom?" Charlie asked him.

"About the way you'd expect. She said I'll never be more than a glorified gardener if I don't go to graduate school. She was not happy with my plans, and she told me to get my ass back to Yale and study architecture the way I was going to, and forget about gardens."

"At least you know where she stands. She sounds like my father sometimes," Charlie said with a wry grin. "So what are you going to do? It's up to you."

Liam hesitated and then smiled at his father. He knew Charlie would back him. "Go to France. I have to give it a try to see if I like it as much as I think I will."

"I think that's a good idea, or you'll always wonder. Who knows?

Maybe you'll end up doing something completely different, and neither one. When do you leave?"

"In two weeks. The doctor says my ankle is healing. He's going to take the pin out before I go. Are you done in the Hamptons, Dad?" He was surprised. Charlie usually stayed until after the Labor Day weekend.

"I'm going back tonight. I had a crisis in the office last week and I had to come back. We worked it out. I'm going back for what's left of August. I'll be back after Labor Day." He had two more weeks left in his rental in East Hampton, and he wanted to spend them with Devon, if she'd see him. It didn't sound like it so far. He hadn't realized the damage he would do by disappearing for a week. He had needed to take some space. He had been so overwhelmed by her it had frightened him afterward. She had a powerful effect on him. But she was more fragile than he had thought. He had fallen in love with her, but he didn't know if he was equal to what she needed from him. And the intensity of their feelings had frightened him. He was afraid to get too attached. He'd been running scared all week. He wasn't sure if he was able to be as consistent as she expected. He had done what he wanted until now. Faye was much sturdier than Devon, and tougher, but she'd had an easy life, parents who adored her and spoiled her, a stable base growing up. Her parents expected a lot of her academically, but she had never been through the traumas Devon had, losing her parents, her husband, and her grandmother. But Devon's vulnerability and tenderness were also part of what he loved about her. He felt bad now that he had upset her so much. He had

The Portrait

thought she would take it in stride the way Faye had, but she hadn't. He didn't know if she would see him again.

Charlie and Liam had breakfast together, and then Charlie left for the office. He was leaving from there at noon, and would get back to the house in the Hamptons between eleven o'clock and midnight.

He thought of Devon again on the flight. He never admitted it, but he knew there was a part of him that never really attached to anyone. He hadn't fully attached to Faye and had gotten away with it. She had never called him on it, or even noticed, but he was well aware that part of the reason their marriage had failed was because he had never really opened up to her, or gotten close to her. Being too close terrified him. And he was already dangerously close to Devon. A marriage counselor he and Faye had seen a few times had recognized his fear of closeness, and he had denied it. Straying with women he didn't care about was easier than seriously committing to his wife. They had been ill-suited, but he had never given the marriage a chance. He'd been cavalier about it and too young to care. And Devon was neither his wife nor some random girl he'd picked up at a party or at a bar. She was a serious woman of value and depth, and she'd paid her dues in life. He wondered if he should just let her go, out of respect for her, or try again. He wasn't sure he was able to open up and make himself truly vulnerable to her, or if he even wanted to. He had no desire to get hurt, or risk immeasurable pain if she hurt him or left him. He had played it safe all his life and protected himself. His mother dying when he was thirteen had left a wound in him that had never healed. The handicaps he had hidden were not so different from Devon's. He was just as scared as she was of it happening again. But he understood now that if Devon saw him again, he had to be real.

They had Wi-Fi on the plane and he wrote her an email, asking her one last time to see him, and walk on the beach with him so they could talk. He promised to leave her alone if she refused again.

She found his email when she came back from a run. She had been thinking about him, and his email sounded more serious than his pleading texts had been. He didn't make excuses for the past week, and he sounded more sincere than he had before. She didn't answer and decided to sleep on it and respond the next day. She didn't want to make a hasty decision, or expose herself to falling for him again and having him repeat the experience that had caused her immeasurable pain.

She went to bed early that night, and Charlie was still thinking of her when he got back to the house. Everything was in order and waiting for him. He found Devon's response when he woke up in the morning. She had given him a meeting place on the beach, neither at his house nor hers. She was willing to meet him on neutral ground at four o'clock. His hopes soared when he read it. He wanted to be brave with her.

She was sitting on the sand when he got there. She was wearing shorts and a white sweatshirt—it was another gray day, which

The Portrait

suited her mood. He looked serious as he approached her and she stood up and met his eyes. She was trying to forget the night she had spent with him, and the wave of love for him he had inspired. What he had done afterward, disappearing for a week, was just as hurtful as their night of lovemaking had been sweet.

They didn't say anything at first, they just walked down the miles of white sandy beach. He was the first to speak after they had walked for a while.

"I'm sorry, Devon. I realize now what I did. I didn't understand how hard it would hit you. I've been coming and going for years without answering to anyone. It's a lousy excuse, and it wasn't nice. Faye never cared if she heard from me or not. That's not a reason to do it to you. I was busy and thoughtless. I probably won't be perfect, but I'll try not to do anything like it again. You've had a lot of loss in your life. That's different. Faye is hard as a rock, she's actually tougher than I am. I don't hear from her either. We had kind of a bond of mutual carelessness about each other. I don't want a relationship like that again either. And thank you for worrying about me when I was being a jerk." She smiled when he said it. "Not everyone dies. Some of us are just stupid and inconsiderate." And scared, but he didn't admit that to her. He would rather she think him careless than cowardly.

"You probably have issues too, losing your mother at the age you did, and your father sending you away to school." She had put her finger right on the wound that was still bleeding though he didn't admit it. It was too frightening to him to even say the words. And even more so because she had understood it without him acknowledging it to her. "And I have one loss you don't know about," she said so softly that he almost didn't hear her in the wind. He turned to look at her, and there was so much pain in her eyes it brought tears to his.

"What don't I know about?" he asked her, afraid of what he'd hear. All the anger had gone out of her, and all he could see was the pain he had caused her for the past week, and something else. He felt deeply remorseful. He wasn't a monster, or unfeeling, even though he had behaved badly for a week.

"You asked me if I have children, and I said no. I had a son, Axel. He was the love of my life, even more than his father. He was a golden child, a wonderful little boy. Two years after my husband died, Axel got meningitis. He was five. He woke up with a high fever and had febrile seizures. I ran to the hospital with him as fast as I could. There was nothing they could do to save him. He died that night. I came to the States after that, because I'd lost him, and I couldn't stay in Paris without him. It was too hard." Charlie was so shocked, he put his arms around her and held her, and she let him. There was nothing he could say to console her. They sat down on the sand, and she looked out to sea, thinking of Axel. It made Charlie realize the burdens she carried deep within her. That was the fragility he sensed more than saw, a wound so deep that nothing could touch it. She had truly been abandoned by everyone she loved, and robbed of their presence in her life. She was a brave woman, even braver than he had known before.

They sat there for a long time, and they walked back slowly to where they had left their cars. He stood looking at her seriously as she got into hers, and spoke solemnly. His respect for her was greater than ever.

The Portrait

"I'll do whatever you want, Devon. I'll leave you alone or we can start over and I'll be more careful next time." She thought he would, but in the long run, she wasn't so sure. She wondered if he was capable of attaching to anyone at a deep level after losing his mother at such a tender age, with a cruel father. Maybe Charlie screwed things up intentionally so no one would attach to him, and he chased away the people who loved him by hurting them. Anything was possible. She didn't have a fast answer for him.

"Why don't you think about it," she said, and he nodded. She drove away a minute later, thinking about Axel and Charlie.

And Charlie drove home, with tears streaming down his cheeks for the son she had lost, and the grief he had caused her.

Charlie visited her the next day at the barn, at her invitation, and they went for a walk on the beach every day. They stayed off painful subjects, and he made her a laugh a few times. And sometimes, they just walked without talking.

By the weekend, she had relaxed, and on Friday night, he took her out to dinner, to the restaurant they had liked the first time they went out. On Saturday night, he brought lobsters to her house and they cooked them together. It was a delicious meal, and they drifted slowly closer again, and she let him spend the night. Their lovemaking was less passionate. It was gentle and tender, with all the feelings he had for her, and she had for him, despite her misgivings about him. He had new respect for her, and deeper compassion. They relaxed with each other and he asked her to spend the Labor Day weekend with him on his boat, and she loved the idea. It was barely big enough for both of them, and had a small cabin. She knew how much he loved the boat. It was a gem, and his prize possession. They were both looking forward to it. He had charted out a number of coves and beaches he wanted to explore with her.

They took off on Friday night, after she helped him load the supplies. She had brought all kinds of treats to eat. He brought wine, and they shared the cooking. She loved where they went. They watched sunsets and sunrises together, and made love in the small bunk. They threw anchor and swam naked off the boat, and he thought he loved her deeply, as much as he could. His marriage ceased to exist for both of them. They felt like they were alone in the world. They came back to the marina on Monday afternoon, and took everything back to his house. Their three days on the boat together were as perfect as it could get, and had swept away the last of the hurt he had caused her. She trusted him again. He was flying back to San Francisco the next day, and she was going back to New York. They spent their last night together at his rented house. She locked up the barn on Monday night, although she came out for a night now and then in the winter.

"What happens now?" she asked him over breakfast on Tuesday morning. They had avoided the subject all weekend. He had a big acquisition deal he was doing in Texas, and an empire to run. She had back-to-back commissions until Christmas. "Will you come to New York?" she asked him. She knew they had a long stretch ahead of them without seeing each other until January, when she did his portrait, if he didn't visit her in New York before that.

"I'll try to get to New York when I can, but it won't be for a

The Portrait

while," he said honestly. She had no break in her schedule either. And she didn't want him to distract her from her commissions. But the three days on his sailboat would feed them for a while. It had been so tender and loving. "And we know we'll have January when I come to sit for the portrait. Maybe we can go somewhere after that." She loved the idea, but it would be a long wait until then. He had let her take dozens of pictures of him on the boat, with the wind on their faces, laughing and talking and working the sails, or at the helm. She loved the images she'd gotten, better than anything she could have taken in the studio, where photos could look so stiff sometimes. She had taken some videos of him too.

They made love one last time before the cars came for them. Hers came first, and Charlie held her tightly in his arms. He had promised to call her this time. He wasn't going to let her slip away from him again, or hurt her. She clung to him for a last minute, fighting back tears, wondering if she really would see him again. "Take care of yourself please," she said softly.

"I promise. You too." She got into the car and he watched her drive away. For the first time in his life he knew he was in love and it terrified him. He didn't want to lose her.

Then he got into his SUV with the driver who was taking him to Teterboro to meet his plane. He thanked the couple who worked at the house, and left them the big tip he gave them every year. He told them he would see them next summer. They liked Devon a lot. She had been very kind to them, polite, warm, and respectful. They hoped he'd bring her back too. They had never seen him with a woman in the ten years he'd come there.

As Devon rode back to New York in the car, she thought about how perfect Charlie was when she was with him. He was terrific, warm and loving and open with her. The big question was if he could maintain it from a distance, or would pull away and run. The danger with him was that closeness terrified him. She knew that now. She understood his demons, and her own. When he hid from her, she felt scared and insecure and abandoned. That was her demon she would have to wrestle with now, and it was a big one. And Charlie suffered from the same thing. In a short time, he had become a powerful force in her life. They had laid everything bare to each other, and now they were going back to their separate worlds. She had no idea if the relationship would survive. He sent her a text while she was still on the road. "Don't forget how much I love you."

"Don't you forget either," she responded to him. The big question, they both knew, was whether he could hold on to her and not run from the risk of losing her as he had his mother. The four months ahead of them were going to be hard, not knowing when they would see each other again.

She got to New York as he got on his plane, and as it took off and headed to California, Charlie had never felt so alone in his life.

She sent him a text then, and he read it and smiled. "I'll be here, waiting for you," she said. He hoped it was true, and that he would have the courage to meet her halfway and trust what they had. As he flew west, as much as he loved her, he wasn't sure. Her love for him terrified him and burned him like a flame and yet he needed her warmth and her love desperately. She was the first woman he had ever truly loved.

Chapter 8

Devon and Charlie both hit the ground running in their respective lives when they got home. Charlie was acquiring more restaurants in half a dozen cities, mostly in the Southwest and Midwest, nowhere near New York. He was racing from one city to another to look at restaurants, to open some and close others. He had bought another company that summer, and was absorbing it into his operation. He was thinking about taking the company public. He had held on to it for a long time, much longer than he'd planned, as it continued to grow exponentially. It was worth several billion dollars now, and it was time to either take it public or sell it. There were advantages and downsides to both and he was weighing it carefully with his financial advisors.

It was hard explaining to Devon what he did every day, and why he was running from one meeting to the next, in cities across the country, with video conference meetings in between. He'd never been busier in his life. And to anyone outside the company, none of it was very interesting. It was all about the mechanics of his business. It was hard to mesh with her schedule, in another time zone. By the time Charlie got free at the end of his day, Devon was asleep in New York. And by the time he got up in the morning, she was already deep in her sittings with her subjects, and couldn't be interrupted. It was the struggle any two people would have had with big careers on opposite coasts, whatever their issues. Because of the time difference and their schedules, most of their communication was by text, which was like eating a handful of pretzels or peanuts instead of dinner. He was always rushing to the next meeting, or she was in a sitting, deep in concentration, communicating with her subject in an intensely focused way. It was harder than either had expected, but they doggedly persisted in writing to each other daily and playing phone tag. It was highly unsatisfactory, but neither of them dared to complain, for fear of upsetting the other. And there was no end in sight. The only clear time they would have together was sitting for his portrait in January. Charlie had thought he would be able to steal a few days to fly back to see her, but he was hit with an avalanche of work, travel, and important decisions to make in September, and October was worse, although he made a real effort to contact her daily, and had been faithful about it. He even worked on the weekends, and so did she. She had a heavy schedule, which was mostly dependent on the overcrowded calendars of her subjects, and she had to accommodate them.

When she read through them sometimes at night, their texts to each other read like fortune cookies. The only homage he still paid to his marriage was spending holidays with Faye and Liam, like Thanksgiving and Christmas, which Devon always spent alone,

The Portrait

working, which lessened the pain of having no family to spend them with. Spending holidays with friends, which she had tried a few times over the years, only shone a spotlight on her losses, and the family she no longer had. Working during the holidays was easier. Liam was planning to come home for Thanksgiving and Christmas, so Charlie would have to be in Atherton with him and Faye.

As busy as Charlie was, it made Devon wonder how they were going to manage in future, living in separate cities at opposite ends of the country. They had the long-distance factor to deal with, and the fact that he was married. The only time he took off all year was in the summer in the Hamptons. She had benefited from the only leisure time he had. He had built a life over the years that sealed everyone out, and allowed him to function like a machine. He loved Devon, and he missed her and wanted to see her, but he was also terrified of the closeness she represented that he wasn't sure he could handle. He was tormented by it constantly, pulled in opposite directions, wanting and needing her, but afraid to become dependent on her and vulnerable. His schedule kept him safe from becoming too involved in her life. It was frustrating for both of them, and he was short-tempered and on edge, which he'd never been before to that degree. In the past he might have been irascible for a few days during a difficult deal. Now he had a short fuse all the time. Even Faye had noticed it, as little as she saw of him. His usual good humor and even disposition had vanished since he'd come home from the Hamptons. Faye, on the other hand, had been happy and relaxed since her two months of downtime in Aspen.

Charlie and Faye ran into each other like people who knew each other meeting at an airport, one Sunday night when he'd had Zoom meetings all day with his offices in Phoenix, Denver, and Atlanta. They hadn't gone as he wanted, and he was in a foul mood when he and Faye collided in the kitchen, to find something to eat in a nearly empty refrigerator. The housekeeper had been sick all week and Faye didn't do grocery shopping. She just ordered in takeout if there was nothing in the fridge. Charlie had just carved out some time to call Devon, who was probably sound asleep. It had gone to voicemail for the second time in two days. She'd been working all weekend to finish a portrait and was drained.

Charlie was staring into the refrigerator, looking annoyed, when Faye walked into the kitchen with a Caesar salad that had just been delivered from her favorite restaurant in Palo Alto.

"Doesn't anybody buy food in this house anymore?" he snapped, "or do we no longer live here?"

Faye noticed the bad mood but didn't react. "Jenny's been out sick all week."

"And buying food is no longer in your job description?"

"I'm management." She grinned at him good-naturedly. "I just ordered a salad from Benito's. I'll split it with you." She took out a plate for him, and divided the salad evenly between them. There was plenty for both of them. She handed him the plate and they both sat down at the kitchen table. Gone were the days when Liam was small and they had shared family meals. It hadn't lasted long. They were never home at the same time, and when they were, Liam preferred eating in front of the TV to sitting between two

The Portrait

warring parents. It was a relief to all of them when they'd stopped. And in his teens, Liam had eaten almost every night with one of his friends' families, which made it easier for his parents.

"What's with you these days?" Faye asked him blandly. "You've been a bear since the summer." He stopped and thought about it, was about to deny it, and looked sheepish. He had been. His questions and fears about the relationship with Devon were tearing him apart.

"I've got too much going on, four acquisitions at opposite ends of the country. I think I want to sell, but we have to get things cleaned up if I go that route. Or an IPO."

"You thrive on that stuff. So what's really eating you?" She was like an old friend now, who knew him well. There was no acrimony left in their relationship. It was just a matter of real estate, and the boardinghouse he stayed at between trips. Devon kept asking him why he couldn't make a detour to New York for a day or two on one of his trips. There was always a reason why he hadn't seen her in almost two months, and had to get back to California for the next meeting. All of the reasons he gave her were valid and plausible. She missed him, but didn't complain. She had a strong work ethic, so she respected his. But his motives weren't entirely pure and he knew it. There was fear in the mix too. He wondered if Faye could guess that he was involved with someone else.

"Are you feeling okay?" she persisted. "Maybe you should see a doctor. A lot of illnesses start with irritability," she said innocently, and he grinned. She was subtle but had gotten the point across. "Like leprosy, for instance. I was reading about it the other day."

"I don't know," he said, hanging his head for a minute. He had come to realize that he had avoided her for their entire marriage. He was tempted to do the same with Devon, to avoid getting hurt. So far he had resisted the urge to run, but the temptation was great, and he had so many excuses not to see her. He and Faye had done the same thing, and had starved their marriage to death, and he had been part of that. Faye didn't need him so she had just given up and moved on emotionally. But Devon did need him and he knew in his heart of hearts that he was avoiding her. "Maybe I'm just turning into an old curmudgeon, like my father," he said, giving himself a hall pass. Faye shook her head.

"That's never going to happen. You don't have it in you. That's not who you are. You're a nice guy. With all due respect—and I liked him for his unvarnished toughness—your father was a genuine sonofabitch. You're not." It was a backhanded compliment and he smiled. "I think you're unhappy about something, whether you admit it to yourself or not."

"Do you ever still wonder what went wrong with us? Did we do it? Did I? Was it destiny, or just a huge mistake all along, and we didn't have a chance?" He wondered lately if his fear of being too attached to anyone had been the cause of their failed marriage.

"I have to admit, I don't think about it a lot anymore, but it was a combination of a lot of things, and who we are."

"Maybe the Elvis cape in Vegas was cursed," he said with a grin.

"To be honest, I was very drunk and my recollection of that moment is pretty dim. But my impression was that you looked more like Liberace than Elvis," she said, and he laughed. "What brought all that up again?" She was curious. The die had been cast long

The Portrait

since—it was way too late to be thinking about what went wrong for them. They had gone on with their lives, and most of the time were at least friends. She hadn't expected more than that from him in years, and she was content, not with him, but with herself. He seemed to be thrashing around, rehashing the past, and tormented over it, if that was really what was bothering him. "Maybe it's time for a change. Maybe you don't want to work like a maniac anymore," she suggested. "It takes a toll. I took my foot off the gas more than usual this summer, and I came back from Aspen feeling great. I'm older than you are, but you've lived ten lifetimes with your business. Maybe that doesn't matter as much as we thought?" He was shocked to hear her say it. She usually worked even harder than he did. "It's hard to have a life and work the way we have until now. Kids leave, marriages end, or your partner dies, and when you retire, what do you have? Nothing, if you have put everything into your business. Don't you want more than that?" she asked him honestly.

"Maybe. But I'm not ready to slow down yet."

"Wait another five years," she said knowingly. "You may get there yet. The people you're running your ass off for now won't remember you twenty years from now."

"I do it for myself," Charlie said firmly.

"That's the trouble. All you have left in the end is you, if that's all you do. That's starting to scare me." It was scaring him too. Everything was these days. Devon, work, his future, his past, the ghosts he had run from for thirty years, and himself. Faye sounded like she was in a much better place than he was. She seemed peaceful, and Charlie was anything but that. He felt as though he had a thousand important decisions to make and had none of the answers. He was at a crossroads, and didn't know which way to turn. He could still have a life, a good life with Devon, or he could keep running and chasing his success, and wind up the way Faye was describing—alone. And if he didn't get back to see Devon soon, that was what would happen. It was inevitable. He was feeling anxious and confused, and running was exhausting.

"It seems like Aspen is good for you," he said kindly, glad that he had run into her, like an old friend.

"It is," she admitted. "I can breathe there. My work here squeezes the life out of me sometimes. It's exciting and exhilarating, but at a hell of a price. At a certain point, how much more money does anyone need? I'm thinking of spending more time in Aspen and working remotely, not all the time, but more than I do now."

"That's a big decision." He was surprised. But she was fifty-four years old, and maybe she wanted to slow down. He was only forty-nine, and at a different point in his life. He wasn't ready to give up the rat race yet, and couldn't imagine it. He loved the high wire and the excitement of what he did. And the power. He was addicted to it, and everything that went with it. In part it was keeping him away from Devon, but what was really keeping him away from her was himself, and his demons. The demons of loss and of closeness and of emotional risk that if you loved someone, you could lose them, just as Devon had. And he had, as a boy. You could lose someone you loved at every age. That's what he was afraid of.

"Well, let me know if you're moving to Aspen," he said. They were more like housemates than husband and wife.

The Portrait

"You'll be the first to know. It's just an idea for now. I really enjoyed the summer. It was hard to come back." It was a first for her.

"Yeah. Me too. Maybe that's why I'm crabby," he said, but she suspected it was something deeper than that, and she had a feeling he knew what was bothering him and he didn't want to tell her. She didn't pry, and pretended to be satisfied with what he told her.

"Any news from our gardener son, by the way?" she asked him.

"He's happy in France. He loves working with the earth and planting something that grows that he can control. You should let that go. He's got to do what he loves, whatever that is. My father never understood that. We know better, we've had careers we love. Not everyone is made for a law career, or a career based on chasing money. He might turn out to be a famous garden designer one day." She couldn't make her peace with it. It was a lot to ask. She was sure he'd regret the decision one day and he was throwing his life away, and his future. "You can talk to him when he comes home for Thanksgiving. I get the feeling he's met a girl he likes in France."

Faye rolled her eyes. "Then we're screwed. He'll never come back."

"He will. He's young," Charlie said indulgently.

"That's what they said about us," Faye added cynically. They were so different but at least they were friends, Charlie mused.

"Thank you for dinner," he said, standing up, and put his plate in the dishwasher. She had eaten hers out of the plastic box. She never bothered to set the table.

"Try not to worry about all of it," Faye said kindly, as he left the

131

kitchen. "Most things take care of themselves." He wished that were true as he went upstairs to his rooms. Faye's were at the opposite end of the house. They had built two master suites years before.

He thought about Devon again as he closed the door to his suite. He missed her, more than he wanted to. She had lodged herself in his heart in a short time, from the very first time he'd seen her. She seemed light-years away in New York.

Devon had been busy from the moment she came back from the Hamptons. She had two days to prepare for her first commission of the fall. He was a famous British actor who had been recently knighted after a long and distinguished career. The portrait was to be hung in his London club and was being paid for by a number of associations. He was well into his seventies, with a distinguished reputation which was well deserved. Sir Reginald Brooke was being painted in white tie, wearing his decoration prominently on his tailcoat. Devon expected him to be stuffy and pompous, and instead found him to be bitingly funny with a keen sense of humor. He was an extremely knowledgeable man on a multitude of subjects. He told her that he researched all his parts intensely for months, and knew the background and history of the characters he portrayed and the kind of lives they would have led.

He had been a Shakespearean actor in his youth, and admitted that he hated Shakespeare with a passion and found him a dead bore. He arrived for the sittings in jeans, a leather jacket, and motorcycle boots, and looked good in them, and changed into his

The Portrait

more formal garb in her dressing room. He was funny and eccentric, brilliant and outrageous. He made the sittings fun. She was painting him with a mischievous smile, almost wicked, with a knowing gleam in his eye, which was how she experienced him while they talked.

"I look a bit naughty, don't I?" he said proudly, when she let him take a look at her progress. She was never mysterious about the work, and didn't mind the subject's feedback most of the time. Now and then it was annoying. She had called him Sir Reginald when they met, and he had said immediately, "*Reggie,* please!" His father, Sir Archibald Brooke, had been a famous Shakespearean actor as well. Reggie had played difficult roles for most of his career, and had won three Oscars in the U.S. His acting was brilliant and as sharp as his mind. He had a quick wit, and told mostly dirty jokes that made her laugh. He didn't attempt to seduce Devon, in spite of her beauty. He had a twenty-eight-year-old wife and two young children. She was Indian, from a very wealthy family in New Delhi, and stunningly beautiful.

Reggie told Devon at the first sitting that he would have found her irresistible and felt honor-bound to seduce her, except that he was completely besotted with his wife, Dahlia, who had him under her spell. He said he felt compelled to explain it so Devon didn't get the incorrect impression that he was gay, which he assured her was not the case. "Old and foolish, and delusional perhaps, but quite straight." He made it all seem funny, and said he had married his wife when she was twenty and he was sixty-eight, and he was the luckiest man in the world. When his wife picked him up after one of the sittings, she was every bit as beautiful as he had said, and appeared to be just as crazy about him. They had just spent a year in New Mexico, while he was shooting a film. They were going back to England for a few months, and then he would be shooting another film in L.A. Devon loved working with him. He had so much personality that the painting was a rich combination of his expressions and the things he had said to her. It came alive the moment one saw it.

Devon finished it in early October, a month after they'd started, and she was sorry when their work together ended. She had really enjoyed painting him.

He had asked her if there was a man in her life in the course of their sittings, and she had answered vaguely that there was someone in California.

"Of course there is," he said, not surprised. "I hope he doesn't leave you alone for long, or he'll miss his chance and someone will snap you up. You're young and beautiful, and one mustn't waste time at your age. It all goes by so quickly. I was a boy yesterday, and now I'm an old man . . . with a beautiful young wife. One has to seize every opportunity. Life is not to be wasted." He had admitted later in their sessions that he had been married four times, always to actresses before Dahlia, and this time he said he had done it right, with a woman of real substance and merit.

He was a perfect example of the kind of subjects she loved to paint, intelligent and interesting with strong characters and fascinating lives and stories to tell.

Her next subject in October was less entertaining. He was the latest judge appointed to the Supreme Court. He had been a controversial choice, but he shared none of his views or life experi-

The Portrait

ence with Devon. He sat silent and serious at every session, and she had to put on music to try to soften his expression. It helped a little but not enough. He had remained rigid and solemn and sealed tight. He had only warmed up in the final sessions, and she managed to get some interesting insights and a wise look in his eyes. But he wanted a stern, exact portrait, which was what emerged in the end. His lack of warmth and exchanges with her made him harder to paint than Sir Reggie, and she had to rely on her training and technique more than her instincts. But the portrait was precisely what he had wanted.

At the beginning of November, she painted a woman who had been a movie star in her youth, had become involved in international relations, and been the U.S. ambassador to England twice, and once to France. The painting was a gift from her to the U.S. Embassy in Paris. She had just been appointed the ambassador to the United Nations. Miriam Holtzman was fascinating and fun to paint, with countless stories about her experiences. She was still beautiful in her late sixties, and had an immense vitality and drive, and strong opinions about international politics. Devon learned a lot from her subjects. The commission had come through the gallery, as most of them did. She liked painting women but had fewer opportunities to do so.

She wanted to tell Charlie about the subjects she was painting, but he rarely had time to talk about it with her. He was rushed and busy, and called her on the fly between meetings. She finished work at five-thirty every day, on the dot, when she released her subjects, which was only two-thirty in the afternoon for Charlie, still in the middle of his workday. He left his own office around eight P.M., and usually went on to business dinners. It was already eleven o'clock at night for Devon, and she was usually asleep by then. She poured so much into the sessions with her subjects that she was drained by the end of the day.

She was painting Miriam Holtzman in a serious black evening gown, with her medals noticeable on her gown. She had been given the Legion of Honor when she left Paris, and was proud of it. She wanted it in the portrait. Each subject had a special request of some kind. Her December subject had already said he wanted to be painted with his dog in the portrait with him. Devon was nervous about it, since a pet could be distracting, and he hadn't specified how big the dog was, but it had been a condition of the commission, and he was an interesting man, so she had agreed.

Liam called his father on the tenth of November, two weeks before Thanksgiving, to tell him that he was working on a project for his classes. He was designing a garden in Normandy, near Deauville, and he couldn't leave it. Thanksgiving wasn't a holiday in France, which Charlie knew, and Liam was really sorry, but he wasn't coming home. He held his breath, while he waited for his father's response, and Charlie hesitated for a minute.

"Is it about your new girlfriend, or school?" Charlie asked him, and Liam was honest with him.

"A little of both, but mostly school. We're working on the project together, as part of a team. I honestly can't leave. They won't like it."

"Your mother will be upset," Charlie said, pensive.

The Portrait

"I know, but all she wants to see me for is to pressure me about Yale again. I'm trying to do what I'm doing here well. I don't want to screw it up. I'm in charge of the project. It looks bad if I leave."

"To your girlfriend or the school?"

"Both. I can deal with her, but I don't want the school to think I'm a flake. Can you deal with Mom?"

"Yes," Charlie said quietly. "But she'll be pissed." However dysfunctional their family, Faye believed strongly in traditions and appearances, and the holidays were sacred to her. She hired caterers to do a beautiful Thanksgiving table and dinner for them every year, just for the three of them. They had no other family and never invited friends. Their disjointed marriage made it difficult to maintain friendships with other couples, and they had lost friends along the way. They had distinctly separate friends.

"I promise I'll come home for Christmas, no matter what. We have off then from school. I'll be home for two weeks. Mom wants me to go skiing in Aspen with her, but I'm going to stay home. I'll be there for sure. Will you tell her for me?" He sounded nervous about it.

"I will. I'm sure you'll hear from her."

"I really can't come home, Dad. It's not a holiday here. They won't get it. It'll count against me."

"I'll take care of it," he promised, but they both knew it wouldn't spare him from his mother's anger and disappointment. Charlie understood.

Charlie told Faye that night, when she came home from the office, and he was home to change for a business dinner. He wanted to call Devon, but he had to deal with Faye first about Liam, and it was already almost too late to call Devon. He was going to miss her again. He hadn't seen her in more than two months, and he knew she was upset. She was getting impatient, and his excuses were wearing thin.

Charlie went down the hall to Faye's bedroom and knocked. She came to the door in a terrycloth bathrobe, fresh from the shower with wet hair. She looked tired, and he had a feeling his announcement was not going to go well.

He got straight to the point. "Liam called me today. Thanksgiving isn't a holiday in France and he can't come home. He thinks it will look bad for him at school if he just takes off. He's working on a project in Deauville. He knows you'll be upset, but he says he really can't come home." Faye exchanged a look with him and was visibly annoyed.

"Is it about the girl?" she asked him directly.

"I think it's really about school, and a little bit of both. Thanksgiving means nothing in France." She pursed her lips but she didn't argue with him.

"I can't force him to come home. What about Christmas?"

"He promised to come home, and I believe him. He'll be here for two weeks. I'm sorry, Faye, I know it means a lot to you."

"It does," she confirmed. "I think once you let the big traditions go, you lose the family completely. I hope he's not planning to stay in France after this class. He needs to come home, before he turns into some half-assed French gardener in a beret." Charlie smiled at the image. She had a way with words.

"He'll be home."

The Portrait

"I wanted him to come to Aspen with me after Christmas. I suppose he won't want to do that either," she said with a sigh.

"He won't want to be with either of us. He'll want to be with his friends. It's the age." She knew it too.

"Is he bringing the girl home for Christmas?" Faye asked, worried.

"He didn't mention it. I doubt it. I don't think it's that serious."

"I hope not. He needs to get his ass back here, like a nice American boy." That remained to be seen, but Charlie wasn't about to tackle that with her now. "What about Thanksgiving for us? It's a little pathetic, just the two of us." She was giving him an opening, and he grabbed for it. He had already thought of it after Liam's call.

"I have some things I need to do in New York. To be honest, I'd rather skip the tradition this year, with Liam not here, and do what I need to do in New York." Faye nodded, thinking about it. She wasn't eager to spend Thanksgiving with him either. It sounded pathetic to her too.

"Do what you have to do," she said. "I'll cancel the caterer, and go to Aspen." She had friends there she would rather be with for the holiday than with him.

"I'm sorry, Faye," Charlie said sympathetically. He could see she was disappointed about Liam. He was too, but he wanted to see Devon.

"It's inevitable with grown kids," she said philosophically, and went back into her bedroom, while Charlie hurried down the hall to call Devon. He hoped she was still awake.

He called her, and the phone rang and finally went to voicemail. She was either not answering or asleep. She didn't go out at night when she was working on a commission. She stayed with it until she finished, and then took a break. She hadn't had many breaks since Labor Day. Her commissions had been back-to-back.

He left her a message and told her he had great news. And then he sent her a text.

"Great news!" he texted her. "If you'll have me, I would like to spend Thanksgiving with you." He thought about it for a minute and then continued, "If you like, I'll try to spend the week. Liam isn't coming home. I'm free!" It was good news. He was excited to see her, but after he sent it, he felt a ripple of fear run down his spine. Spending a major holiday with her was a big statement. He was getting in deeper, but it was the perfect opportunity to see her, and she had been patient for two and a half months. If he loved her, he needed to go. He felt torn between wanting her and needing to see her and his fear of getting too dependent on her, and too deeply attached. He sat staring at his phone for a few minutes after he sent the text.

He pushed his fears aside. He was going to see her again at last, almost three months after they had left each other in the Hamptons. The time had flown, and in spite of his demons and scars of the past, he knew that she was the love of his life. She was a wonderful person, and there was nothing to fear.

Chapter 9

Charlie boarded his plane on the Sunday before Thanksgiving with a strange mixture of trepidation and excitement, like a child before Christmas who is half afraid that some of his mischief through the year may have counted against him, but who has an overriding faith that Santa wouldn't let him down. There was no denying or changing the fact that he hadn't seen Devon in eleven weeks, almost three months, way too long not to see the woman he loved, and who loved him. Devon had been remarkably restrained and reasonable about it, but it had been much longer than he had planned. He had been working nonstop on complicated deals and business problems since Labor Day, with some important decisions to make, about whether to sell the company or not. Somehow day-to-day life wore him down, and in spite of having his own plane at his disposal, he hadn't made it to New York.

She had been busy too, and had just finished her portrait of the ambassador to the United Nations, and she said it had come out extremely well and the subject was pleased. She had done nothing but work since she'd last seen him, but between being married and being busy, Charlie hadn't brought a lot to the table in recent months. He didn't say it to Devon, but he felt guilty. He needed to see her. They had known each other for such a short time that he wanted to see her and make sure he still loved her as much as he thought. She seemed very stable and constant, and he had been very good about calling and texting her this time, and not abandoning her, although their conversations were usually short, rushed between meetings, and his texts equally so. They were barely more than a few words and an emoji of a kiss or a heart. She was thrilled that they were going to spend a week together. He had cleared his schedule for the entire week. Faye was in Aspen, Liam in Paris. He had no family to spend the holiday with, so he was giving it all to Devon. He thought it would be interesting to see how they got along, living at her place for a week. It was a more formal setting than the barn in East Hampton, and it would be a slice of real life, which he wanted to share with her. She was ecstatic he was coming, and had asked him dozens of questions about what he liked to eat for breakfast, if he wanted to go to the theater, or whether to make restaurant reservations for them. She treated him like a homecoming hero, or a husband, which was unfamiliar to him. Faye never asked him what he wanted, and they never went out to dinner together. That was ancient history for them. With Devon, everything felt bright, shiny, and new, with the feel of first love. It almost felt like he was moving in.

He had his own apartment on Fifth Avenue, which was more

like a hotel suite than a home. Hers was where she actually lived and worked. It meant a lot to her to have him stay with her there. She wanted him to feel welcome and pampered. He was touched by the effort she was making. He had said that he loved her, so this was what happened between normal people when they fell in love and the relationship progressed. He had forgotten or never known what that was like. Faye had never been that attentive, even in the beginning. It was more familiar to him to be ignored.

Devon had thought about it and made a decision before he came. She was not going to complain about the three months since she had last seen him. She was going to make it so comfortable and homelike for him to be there that he would want to come back, hopefully sooner in the future than the time between now and their last meeting in the Hamptons. It had been a long time, and it had been hard. But his frequent contacts, however brief, had reassured her that he wasn't abandoning her, he was just busy, which was inevitable with a man as important as Charlie. She believed that he hadn't had time to come to New York, and she had been valiant about it. The three portraits she had completed had kept her busy and filled her time. She was starting her last commission of the year the Monday after Thanksgiving. It was for a famous American movie star who already had a sizable collection of portraits of himself, and loved having them done. He had said that his collection wasn't complete without one by Devon Darcy, and he couldn't wait to sit for her. She intended to finish it by Christmas, take a break, and get ready to do Charlie's portrait in January. She was keeping the whole month free for him, and was booked solid for February and March. She would be doing portraits of a well-known senator and two women, a great philanthropist and a writer. She loved the variety of subjects she painted, but the one of Charlie was the one she most wanted to do. Her whole heart would be in it, and she already had some thoughts about the right look and background, but she wanted to hear his ideas too.

She filled her apartment with flowers the day before he came, had everything spotlessly clean and in perfect order. She'd made reservations at the restaurants he requested, had her hair trimmed, gotten a manicure and pedicure. She was ready for visiting royalty, and more precisely the love of her life. She had stocked the refrigerator with things she had noticed he liked to eat, including a tin of caviar she had bought for Thanksgiving. She was going to cook the turkey herself, and had been reading recipes for stuffing. She had bought all the traditional trimmings, and ordered pies at her local bakery in the Village.

When the plane landed at Teterboro, Charlie stopped at his apartment first to pick up some things he thought he'd need and hadn't bothered to bring—a bathrobe, a razor and toothbrush, a pair of slippers—and then stopped at a florist to buy Devon an enormous bouquet of flowers. He noticed that the city was already being decorated for Christmas, and the West Village had a warm, friendly neighborhood feeling to it when he got out of the car with his usual driver, and rang her doorbell. He smiled when he heard her voice on the intercom, and all his anxious misgivings were forgotten. She opened the door in black velvet pants and a red sweater, and he pulled her into his arms and instantly remembered what he had been missing and how much he loved her. All doubt was swept away on a river of love that carried them both along.

The Portrait

The driver and Devon helped him carry his things upstairs into her apartment and to her bedroom on the upper floor. He had never been in her apartment, and he saw all the beautiful things she had collected, her paintings hanging, candles lit, and soft music playing, and he felt as though he was in a magical place. As soon as the door closed on his driver, Charlie's passion for her overflowed, and they raced up the stairs to her bedroom to make love. Her bedroom felt like a cocoon that enveloped him, and her bed like a cloud. He wondered how he had stayed away from her for as long as he had. Clearly, he had forgotten how bewitching she was, and how beautiful, and how amazing their lovemaking was. Several hours later, he put on his bathrobe and they wandered downstairs to the kitchen. She made toast, chopped an egg, sliced lemons, and served the caviar in a crystal bowl on a silver platter instead of saving it for Thanksgiving. Everything was perfect and beautiful, and arranged to make him feel welcome and at home. He felt like royalty.

He walked into her studio and was in awe of her recent paintings. She showed him photographs of the three portraits she had done since she'd last seen him, and he was stunned by how beautiful they were. He couldn't wait to sit for his in January.

She had cold chicken in the fridge and they made pasta and a salad, ate dinner, and finished the caviar.

"You are going to get me so spoiled I will never want to leave," he said, eating by candlelight in her kitchen. "I missed you so much," he said in a husky voice filled with emotion. They put the dishes in the dishwasher and the leftovers in the fridge, and went upstairs to sit in the cozy den off her bedroom. The apartment wasn't large but it was warm and welcoming. His house in Atherton was much bigger and more of a showplace, but it was cold, while Devon had given her home her own special, inviting, eclectic vibe. It was the home of an artist, and a sensitive woman who loved beautiful things. She looked perfect in her natural habitat, and he fell in love with her all over again.

They went out the next day to walk around the Village. He liked the friendly chaotic jumble of her neighborhood, with restaurants, gourmet food stores, and high-end vintage shops with Vuitton trunks in the window. It felt inviting and informal, and he loved it. They made love before lunch when they went back to her apartment, saw a movie in the afternoon, and went skating that night in Central Park, their taxi driving them past the tree at Rockefeller Center on the way home. It was an entirely New York experience, but different from any he'd had before. He came to the city as a businessman to work there, and came and went quickly. He hadn't tasted the life of a New Yorker, and she did everything to make it enjoyable for him. They had dinner at The Grill and Le Bernardin, as he had requested, and they made love anytime they felt like it.

Devon got up early on Thanksgiving morning to put the turkey in the oven, and when Charlie woke up as he heard her stirring, they made love. She set a beautiful table for the meal, with delicately embroidered linens that had been her grandmother's. Everything she touched was beautiful and thoughtful and meant to please him, and he suddenly had tears in his eyes as they sat down to their Thanksgiving meal and a memory flashed through him. She had folded the napkins into swans, and he looked at her as though he had seen a ghost, or been visited by one.

The Portrait

"My mother used to do the napkins that way on Thanksgiving. She taught me how to do it, and I used to help her set the table." He unfolded one, and redid it correctly from a deep memory he had long forgotten. His fingers remembered how to do it more than his mind. For an instant, he wondered if his mother had sent Devon to him. His mother had loved all the same elegant, genteel things that Devon did. He had married a woman who had no interest at all in elegance or gracious homemaking, who hired a caterer because she couldn't be bothered, and his father hadn't cared about the little touches his wife had provided, but Devon did all of it. She had arranged a beautiful bouquet of flowers for the table, which Charlie's mother would have done too.

"She was very artistic. She used to paint landscapes," he said, remembering that too. "I still have one somewhere. My father didn't like seeing it, it upset him, and he told me to put it away."

The dinner they had made together was delicious, and they walked to Washington Square and back again afterward, and watched a favorite old movie they both loved that night and made popcorn. Without knowing it, Devon had provided all the little thoughtful touches that his life had been missing, all his life, since his mother's death, doing everything his wife should have done for him, and didn't. Devon had restored what was lost, and given him his fair due, and he was overwhelmed with all the tender sensations of joy and gratitude that it brought up in him.

"You are the most perfect woman I have ever known," he whispered to her after the movie, and they made love again.

They went to see the tree at Rockefeller Center on Friday night, which was decorated but not lit yet. Then they went for a drink at the Plaza, and he took her for a hansom cab ride in Central Park, which was corny but wonderful as they snuggled under a blanket and kissed as it started to snow.

They had a Chinese dinner afterward, and saved their fortunes from the cookies. His said "A very good year ahead," and hers said "Good things are going to happen." And then they went home, which felt like home to him now too. It was easy to settle into the magic of the world she created around her, and included him in. He felt happy and peaceful and relaxed, and as though he was finally in the right place. He had called Liam on Thanksgiving, and Faye had sent him a text that said just "Happy Thanksgiving," and though he was sure she had sent it to her entire address book, and not particularly to him, he sent her the same generic greeting. It had been the best Thanksgiving of his life. The hansom cab ride in the snow was the most romantic moment. The horse was white with a purple blanket draped over it and its owner wore a top hat. Devon felt like the princess in the fairy tale with him again.

They took a long walk around Central Park on Saturday, and wandered in and out of a few stores, which were crowded on the holiday weekend, and then they walked all the way back down to the Village. He was leaving the next day, and they were both trying not to think about it. The good news was that he would be back in the first week of January for his portrait, so she would only have five weeks without him this time, not eleven. He was spending Christmas in Atherton with Faye and Liam. Devon had invited him to come for New Year's Eve with her, but he wasn't sure of his plans yet, and he wanted to spend time with Liam before he went back to France. She had to accept her role in his life in second

The Portrait

place after his son, and sometimes his wife. She didn't complain, she accepted it gracefully, and was grateful for the week they had just shared. She couldn't ask for more than that. Everything about it had been perfect, for both of them. Charlie was in awe of the magic she had created, and the home she made for him while he was there.

They made love that night and the next day before he left. Her eyes were sad when he kissed her, and so were his. He had a heavy heart, leaving her. He didn't want to go. He wanted to stay there in her arms and her bed and her warm cozy home forever.

"See you in January," he said in a hoarse voice, fighting back tears. "Thank you for every minute of this week." He thought of the swan napkins again but couldn't say it. She had given him a cherished memory of the past, and memories for the future to keep him warm. She had given him everything beyond what he could have dreamed of. He kissed her before he got in the car.

"I love you," he whispered. There was nothing else to say. She had done and said it all, and she stood smiling and waving on the sidewalk in a pink fuzzy sweater as he drove away, with his heart aching, as he tucked it all into his pocket like a string of bright beads that would remind him of each moment.

He looked strangely sober as he boarded the plane. It was late afternoon and it was dark. Her light had shone so brightly for the entire week. As the plane took off, he thought of the napkins again. He remembered his last Thanksgiving with his mother, the flowers on the table, the swan napkins, a beautifully embroidered tablecloth like Devon's grandmother's. All the little touches that Devon did so naturally and so well, and it was like an omen that the same fate would befall her as his mother. He couldn't bear it, losing another person like her. She was too perfect for this world. She loved him too much, and he knew that if something bad happened to her, he couldn't save her either. One day she would die, just like his mother had. He had his phone in his hand and he wanted to thank her for an exquisite week, but he felt as though his fingers were frozen and he couldn't. He couldn't write her anything. He just stared out the window at the clouds they were flying through and the night sky above them. There were tears running down his cheeks, as he thought of Devon and his mother. He closed his eyes in a pain he hadn't felt in years. He stared out the window for a long time, with a feeling of terror and despair, and then he fell asleep, and woke when they landed in San Francisco. He hadn't eaten dinner or watched a movie. He was going to send Devon a text, thanking her, but as he slipped his phone into his pocket, he knew he couldn't.

Chapter 10

When Charlie got to the house in Atherton, it was dark and empty. Faye wasn't coming home until the next day. It was a relief to find no one there in the silent house. His feelings were raw and his heart was aching. He felt fear engulf him like tar, and he lay down on his bed in the dark. It was late in New York by then, one in the morning, and he couldn't call Devon to hear her voice—she would be asleep by then. He was back in the real world, his world, a world without warmth or love or feelings or anyone to spoil him who could disappear tomorrow.

He understood how to live in his world. It was like the plastic box Faye's salads came in—empty and transparent and functional. He didn't know how to exist in Devon's world, a universe of grace and beauty and warmth and love. It was like being in heaven, and being cast into hell afterward, as he landed back on earth.

She texted him the morning after he arrived. She was worried, he could tell. She had expected to hear from him—they had been so close for eight days, so fused together like one person, one soul, one vision of life, in harmony with each other. "Did you get home okay? I miss you. I love you, D," it said. He read it and didn't answer her. He felt paralyzed, unable to speak or communicate, as though she had cast a spell on him that condemned him to a silent darkness without her, and he didn't know how to escape, or break the spell.

She texted him at his lunchtime, and again when she finished work. He read the texts as though they were written by someone he didn't know. But the person he didn't know was himself. He was lost in a frightening darkness, where he could see nothing, hear nothing, do nothing, and was alone. He was in agony, and had to go through the motions in his office, pretending that life was normal, when there was nothing normal about it.

He had been cast into a hell ruled by fear and was hiding from his demons. At every turn, they would find him.

Faye came home from Aspen that night, and found his door closed and locked when she got home.

"How was New York?" she shouted through the door on the way to her room.

"Fine," he answered. "How was Aspen?" He could speak when he had to. The demons would let him.

"Cold as hell and gorgeous," she answered. "The lifts are already open. I got in a couple of good runs."

"Great," he said, praying she'd leave him alone, and she did, and went to unpack. He didn't see her in the morning, which was a blessing. He couldn't bear talking to her or anyone else. Devon called again that day, and he didn't take the calls. He didn't know

The Portrait

what had happened to him, except he did. He could live in the icy, empty, dead environment of his marriage to Faye, but the tenderness and deep love that Devon lavished on him, with every minute kind and loving gesture, ripped him wide open, and his guts were all over the floor and he couldn't get them back in. All his feelings and fears were on fire and laid bare. She had broken him open like a child's piggy bank for the pennies he had inside. He was emotionally bankrupt, and he knew it. His mother had taken his ability to love another human with her. His father had frozen the little that was left. The demons had eaten him alive and left only hair and bones instead of a whole person. He wasn't whole, he knew it now. He couldn't even fake it. He had nothing to give her. He was nothing, except the cardboard person who had lived with Faye for twenty-three years. She expected nothing from him, and gave him nothing in return. If she had been more like Devon, they would have gone up in flames even sooner. He hungered for everything Devon had to give him, but he couldn't tolerate it. His wounds were too raw, his heart too damaged.

He thought of their lovemaking and how easy it had been because of her. She made it so easy to love her. For so many years he had slept with women he didn't care about, as a form of physical exercise with no soul to it, and with Devon he came to life again, and then died when it was over. He felt like a robot whose wiring was all screwed up, and no one could fix it.

Devon kept calling day after day, and his heart ached every time he saw her texts and messages, and after a week she gave up. He silently begged her forgiveness, and hoped she would recover quickly from the pain he was inflicting on her, but he knew it would be far worse if he stayed with her, for both of them, when she discovered that he was only the shell of a man, with nothing inside. Now she knew, and she could walk away and recover. He wanted her to forget him as soon as she could. He knew the pain he was causing her, and he ached for her, but his fears were more powerful than his compassion and his love, and his terror was in full control. He was powerless against his fears and the cruelty they made him commit. Knowing it only made it worse. He hated himself for it, while still loving her.

When Charlie didn't send her a text from the car or when he got on the flight, Devon thought he had fallen asleep. They'd had late nights with their lovemaking, and run around all day, and gone out in the evenings. She was tired too, but it had all been so magical and perfect she felt like she was flying.

The next day, she imagined him at meetings. She kept trying. She doggedly kept calling, thinking he was swamped. By the end of the second day, she had a sick feeling in her stomach. By the third day, panic had set in. She didn't understand. What had happened? Had she said something? Done something? They had both been so happy. The fourth and fifth days were a blur. And then she knew, on the sixth day. He was never going to call her again. He had run, as fast and as far as he could. She was never going to see him or hear from him again.

It was like a death, an agony she knew so well, where nothing makes sense and you want to run the film again and again to see where it went wrong. Whatever the reason, whatever excuse he

The Portrait

allowed himself to use, he had cut her out of his life. She felt like he had killed her. He had stabbed her a thousand times in the heart, a million, like a crazed attacker who had to destroy her, and he had. She had trusted him this time, which made it even worse. She had nothing to protect her from the blows or the pain. Her soul was bleeding. She had a commission to do and she could hardly get through the days. As it became clear to her that he was never going to see her again, or speak to her, or respond, it nearly brought her to her knees, and she had to pretend to function and concentrate on the painting to survive.

She had been through it before with Jean-Louis and Axel and her grandmother. But she wasn't painting portrait commissions then. She was in school, or doing little projects. It took a monumental effort to pay attention to the painting she was working on. Fortunately the subject was very nice and easy to work with. He had brought his dog with him, a giant bullmastiff who looked like he could kill a man in one bite, and thought he was a lapdog. He tried to sit on her lap several times, and licked her face. He added some comic relief to an otherwise grim picture. She felt like her heart was going to fall out of her chest every day. She felt dizzy and sick to her stomach. Charlie had done it again. He had abandoned her. First he had come as close to her as was humanly possible and let her think that he loved it too, and then with one cruel lethal gesture, he had flung her off a cliff onto the rocks below, and killed her.

She was in agony every minute of every day, keening for him, pining for him, remembering each moment they had spent together and how perfect it had been. And now he was punishing her for it. As sweet as it had been, he needed to make it that much more brutal now. She felt like she was dying. And hoped she would soon. She couldn't stand the pain of the loss for much longer. He had abandoned her, again.

After a week, she hoped he might wake up and come to his senses and contact her, but he didn't. She didn't reach out to him again—there was no point. She used every fiber of her being to concentrate on the painting she was supposed to do, before the subject accused her of being a fraud, sued her or demanded his money back, and destroyed her reputation. She had gotten a good beginning on the dog, but she hadn't even begun to sketch his owner. And for once, she didn't allow him to see her progress, or lack of it. She painted all day and got nothing.

And at night, after he left her apartment, she lay in bed and cried herself to sleep. It was a vicious circle of tears and torment day after day, and night. She had been there before and it was agonizingly familiar. He brought all the other deaths and losses back in vivid memory. Even Axel.

It took all of Charlie's strength not to call her or answer her texts, and when they stopped, he was worried about her. If anything ever happened to her, no one would know to call him. He couldn't bear the thought of something happening to her. He didn't know what to do to get her out of his head. She lived there now, constantly, taunting him, reminding him of how wonderful it had been with her. He wanted her out of his life now, for her sake. He was determined not to contact her again. He wondered if being

The Portrait

with a woman would help. What the French called "chasing one nail with another."

He went to a bar in Palo Alto one night, when Faye was out with clients, so she didn't see him leave. It was a bar where loose women were known to hang out. The men in the office swore that if you wanted to get laid, you should go to that particular bar, and within half an hour, you'd be all set. He drove there from the house in Atherton, walked up to the bar and ordered a double Johnny Walker Black Label on the rocks, drank it in five minutes, and ordered another.

"Tough day at the office?" the bartender asked, wondering if he'd gotten fired. He drank like it. He took a little more time with his second drink, and a pretty blonde with huge implants and a very short skirt and stilettos came and stood next to him at the bar, eyeing him coyly. She looked cheap but willing, which was all he needed. He wasn't sure if she was a pro or not, and didn't care. He was usually more discerning about the women he picked up, but all he wanted was someone to get Devon out of his head so he wouldn't think of her every hour of the day and night and remember her gentle, sensual touch, or exquisite body and her green eyes, which haunted him.

"Would you like a drink?" Charlie asked the blonde, without feeling guilty. She was no innocent. And neither was he. There was a time when he regularly slept with women he picked up at bars. He hadn't in a long time. And they had always been ordinary women, not hookers.

"Sure." She ordered a wine spritzer, and whispered to him. "Did you drive here or come in an Uber?" He didn't see what difference it made.

"I drove," he said, almost finishing his Scotch.

"Wanna go out to your car and have some fun?" she asked him, batting her fake eyelashes at him, and he decided to go through with it. This was what he had come for.

"Let's do it," he said, taking a last swallow of the Johnny Walker, and she took a long sip of her spritzer and followed him outside to his car. He unlocked it and got into the backseat with her. He had parked at the far edge of the parking lot under a streetlamp, which was convenient. She looked at him hesitantly for an instant.

"Do you mind giving me a hundred?" she asked him. "I want to get my hair done tomorrow." So she was a hooker, or maybe an amateur. He pulled out his wallet and handed her two fifty-dollar bills, and she stuffed them in her overburdened bra, as he watched her, and felt her unzip his pants and reach in to free him, and suddenly the reality of what he was doing and his desperation hit home, and he gently grabbed her wrist and stopped her. He didn't know if she was going to give him a blow job or a hand job, but he didn't want to find out. He was drunk, but not enough to be paying a hundred dollars for a blow job in a parking lot when there was a woman in the world who loved him. He felt crazy, but saner than he had been when he walked her to his car.

"It's all right," she said soothingly, "don't be embarrassed. I'm a nice girl. I teach school."

"I don't know if that's true or not, but whatever you do, you shouldn't be doing this. I'm a mess but I'm a decent guy. One night you're going to come across some guy who'll beat the shit out of

The Portrait

you or kill you." He zipped up his pants, reached for his wallet again, and gave her another hundred. "I'm sorry. Now call an Uber and go home."

"Are you sure? I could go all the way for two hundred."

"I probably couldn't after two double Scotches. I was having some kind of a meltdown, but this isn't the solution." He stepped out of the car and she followed him, looking puzzled. "Do you want me to call you an Uber?" he asked her. Under the streetlight, he could see that she was very young, maybe eighteen or twenty, and he felt sorry for her.

"Yeah, sure, that's nice of you. Thank you," she said, as they stood there and he called the Uber on his phone, and it arrived five minutes later.

"Take care," he said, as she got in the car and waved at him, and it drove away. He got behind the wheel of his car and drove home, feeling like he had been insane. What if he'd gotten arrested, or if she really was a hooker and stabbed him and killed him for his watch and his wallet?

He had another glass of Scotch and went straight to bed. He didn't look at his phone for messages from Devon. He didn't know what he dreaded most, another message from her, or none.

He called Adam Stein when he woke up in the morning, on his private line. Adam picked up, and Charlie sounded raw. He remembered the night before all too clearly.

"Do you have time for lunch with me today?" he asked.

"Sure. What's the problem? Something wrong?" Adam already had a lunch, but he was going to cancel it for Charlie when he heard the way he sounded.

159

"I think I'm losing my mind. I need to talk to someone, a friend."

"Sure. Why don't you come to my office. I'll order in. Better than a restaurant. How about twelve-thirty?"

"Thank you. I'll see you then." Charlie hung up, took a long hot shower, and didn't go into the office. Faye had left early for a meeting, and he was grateful not to see her, or anyone else.

He drove to the city, parked his car, and walked along the Embarcadero for a while, looking at the bay and the seagulls and the boats, trying to find firm ground under his feet again. He felt as though he'd been roller-skating on marbles since he got home from New York, from being with Devon.

Charlie arrived at Adam's office five minutes early, eager to see him. The receptionist told him to go in. He knew where to find Adam, in the big corner office. He had an enormous glass desk and wood-paneled walls, and a breathtaking view of the bay, looking east to the Bay Bridge. The view was more industrial than on the Golden Gate side, which was residential. He stared mournfully across the desk at Adam. Charlie looked woebegone, with dark circles under his eyes. Adam was worried just looking at him.

"Is someone suing you?" he guessed.

"No."

"Sexual harassment?" Charlie shook his head, thinking of the night before.

"I almost got a blow job in a parking lot from a hooker last night. I didn't but that's when I figured I should call you or a shrink, or both." Adam was his closest friend as well as his lawyer. They had gone to grade school together. They'd grown up together. "I feel crazy. I met a woman this summer. She's everything I could ever

The Portrait

want. Smart, beautiful, talented, successful. She's a famous artist, a painter. She's a wonderful person, kind, decent. She's everything Faye isn't, and never was, even when we liked each other."

"And she wants money. She's blackmailing you," Adam guessed.

"Not at all. She doesn't want anything from me. She just wants to spoil me and love and treat me like the hero in a fairy tale." He looked miserable when he said it.

"And Faye wants everything you own in a divorce?"

"Probably. But she doesn't know."

"Do you love this woman?" Adam looked at him intently. Charlie didn't look crazy. He looked shattered, broken.

"Desperately. I love everything about her. She's perfect for me. I spent time with her in the Hamptons this summer, and I just spent a week with her in New York. She lives there. I left her the Sunday after Thanksgiving, and I haven't answered her messages since."

"Why? Is she married?" Adam was trying to figure out where the problem was, and he couldn't so far.

"She's a widow. She's lost everyone she ever loved. Her parents when she was a kid, her husband, her son, her grandmother. She's alone. But I can't do it. I can't. She reminds me of my mother. What if the same thing happens to her? Faye and I don't love each other, we never did. I realize now that I've never been attached to anyone for my whole adult life, except Liam. What if I love this woman? If I make a life with her, and she leaves me, or something happens to her and she dies? I don't think I'd survive it. I think after my mother died, at some gut level I decided never to love anyone again. And I haven't. It's all been superficial, women I don't care about and don't love, who don't love me, and Faye, who'd be fine if I keeled over dead tomorrow. We live together like strangers. It works for me. I'm closer to the guy who mows my lawn. But this woman, I would die if something happened to her."

"So what are you doing about it?" Adam asked him.

"I walked out on her. I abandoned her for the second time. She's better off without me."

"I agree with your analysis. Your mother was such a lovely person that I was traumatized when she died. My mother took me to a shrink, because I was terrified my own mother would die after that," Adam said.

"My father sent me away, and I haven't loved anyone since, except my son. And he's independent and not a big risk-taker. But if I stay with this woman and I love her, which I do, and something happens to her, it would kill me. I can't take the chance. I ran," he said with tears in his eyes, "and I'm still running. I ditched her. I haven't contacted her since I left New York, after we spent the most incredible week of my life together."

"You can't run away from love forever," Adam said seriously, worried about his friend. "Maybe she'd outlive you. She's not going to die because your mother did—and look at the life you live with Faye. You're like strangers. I'm closer to my barber than you are to your wife." They both knew it was true, and Faye would have agreed.

"There's no risk factor like that. Nothing hurts."

"It's like being dead. You can't run away from this woman because you love her, that's insane."

"That's how I feel. Crazy. All I want to do is be with her, and I'm scared to death to be dependent on her, and too attached to her. I

The Portrait

have freedom now. I do what I want. I don't owe anyone explanations. I don't care about anyone except Liam. And her."

"Charlie, that's not a life. You'll be alone forever if you don't take a chance."

"I thought I would be and it was fine. Until I met her. She must hate me by now. I disappeared on her for a week this summer, and it nearly killed her. She must feel even worse now."

"You have to deal with this. You're sane about Liam, why can't you be sane about her?"

"Maybe because she's a woman. I thought I could save my mother and I couldn't. I tried to make all kinds of deals with God."

"I remember how it was. It was awful," Adam said, still moved when he thought about Charlie's mother. He still remembered her distinctly, and how sick she had gotten so quickly, and then she died. "You can't live like you do with Faye forever," Adam said firmly. "Would you divorce her?"

"She'd take half of everything I have. Faye isn't famous for being merciful, or fair. She likes money."

"We all do. You can afford to give her a hell of a lot." Charlie had always been generous. "Your freedom is worth it."

"I'm not sure Devon would even speak to me by now. It's been two weeks. And she doesn't take abandonment lightly. She's been badly wounded, especially when she lost her son. He was five."

"What's her name?" Adam asked, curious. He pulled his computer toward him as Charlie told him, and he googled her. He found her immediately and stared at her. "Oh my God, Charlie . . . she's amazing. She has credentials a mile long. Important ones. She's painted everyone but the pope."

"She was supposed to do my portrait in January for the bank," which would be impossible now. They'd have to cancel the commission.

"To hell with the bank. You have to get sane about this. She's not your mother, you're not thirteen, and she's not going to die . . . not soon, anyway. Why don't you go back to New York and talk to her. Or at least call her."

"I don't even know if she'd see me by now."

"If she loves you, she would. What are your options? A life with a woman you don't love whom you barely speak to and getting blow jobs from hookers in parking lots, or a real life with a woman who loves you?" He made it sound as bad as it was, and Charlie looked depressed. "You cannot run out on this woman because your mother died. This woman is alive and loves you, from what you say."

"I'll think about it," Charlie said. He hadn't touched the sandwich Adam had ordered for him, and he looked sick with grief and worry.

He stayed for a few more minutes and then he left. He went to his office and looked unhappy for the rest of the day. Everything Adam had said made sense. But Charlie was terrified of getting attached to anyone, especially Devon, because he loved her so much.

He promised himself he would call her by Christmas. That was the best he could do for now. And by Christmas, who knew if Devon would speak to him. Christmas was twelve days away.

Chapter 11

Brandon Yates was one of the most entertaining subjects Devon had ever painted. She was deeply depressed by Charlie abandoning her again. Especially after the magical week they had spent together, which made it doubly hard. It was clear to her now that every time they got close he would run away from her. She understood now why he did it, but it wasn't going to get any better. He couldn't help it. And she couldn't help him. He wouldn't let her. He was incapable of being close to anyone, especially Devon, because she loved him. The relationship was doomed, and she was mourning it silently while she worked on Brandon Yates's portrait. He was so good-looking he wouldn't be hard to paint—even the sketches of him that she did before using paints were handsome. He said he wanted a Gothic mood to the portrait, which threw her at first. He showed up with a full suit of armor he wanted to wear at the sitting. They talked about it, and she suddenly had an idea. In a storeroom full of unusual objects that she sometimes used to create a mood or a counterpoint to a painting to give it additional interest, she had a miniature eighteenth-century vermeil suit of armor that had been used to sell armor to aristocrats, as samples of the armorer's wares. It was beautifully made, with silver trim and elaborate engraving. She showed it to Brandon and he loved it.

"Where did you get that? It's fantastic."

"I bought it at an auction in Paris," she said, pleased that he liked it. She suggested they put a table next to him with the helmet of the armor he'd brought, and the miniature armor, which made an interesting composition, and gave it a personal touch. She offered to paint him in a Gothic-style chair, with the still life next to him, and his dog on the other side. The giant bullmastiff looked somewhat Gothic too. "And I can paint a fabulous collar on him." The dog's name was Thornton, and he rolled over on his back with all fours in the air whenever he wanted attention. He had a teddy bear he took everywhere, and he put his paws on Devon's shoulders and licked her face.

"He likes you," Brandon said, pleased. He was interesting and eccentric, with a tremendous talent. He also wrote and directed and produced his own movies. He told her funny stories that made her laugh, about movies he had shot on location. He was the only thing that made her life bearable once she realized that Charlie had abandoned her again, and the romance was over. She was heartbroken, but she was a consummate professional and didn't let it show. Once or twice Brandon caught her in the kitchen crying and blowing her nose.

"I'm sorry," she said, apologizing, and pulled herself together

The Portrait

until he left after the sitting. He was kind and sympathetic and funny.

"Don't be. Whoever the guy is, he's an asshole if he makes you cry." She laughed.

"You're right." He invited her out to dinner after the second sitting and she declined. "I never socialize with my subjects," she explained, and Brandon looked surprised.

"Why not? I sleep with most of my leading ladies. Only the good-looking ones, actually. It creates an additional bond and gives credibility to the love scenes," he said in a matter-of-fact way that made her smile.

"Socializing with my subjects distracts me. And I spend a lot of time sketching after the sittings, so I get the bone structure right."

"I never thought about that," he said pensively. "Devon, how many commissions do you do a year, for portraits?" She thought about it.

"Ten or twelve."

"How many are women?"

"Two or three a year. Men are usually more eager to have portraits done than women. And I'm better known for the men I paint."

"All right, so that gives you seven or eight men a year to pick from. If you slept with most of them, you wouldn't have time to care about the jerk who's had you crying every day I've been here." She laughed, though she suspected he meant it. She hadn't slept with eight men in her entire lifetime, and didn't want to.

"What if they all make me cry?" she teased, as she took photographs of him to use later if she needed them for reference of a detail, like a chin or an ear.

"In that case, you're definitely picking the wrong subjects. First of all, no old or ugly ones. You should only pick subjects you find attractive personally. No one in religious orders, like the pope—they won't sleep with you, which wastes your time. Take me, for instance. If you sleep with me, you'll have a hell of a good time. I'll make you laugh, take you to expensive dinners and some really great parties, and when it's all over we'll be friends forever. I always stay friends with the women I have affairs with. My leading ladies love me, for the duration of the movie. You should think about it," he said, appearing to be serious, while she tried to concentrate on the photographs and videos she was taking. "And you would completely forget the idiot who upset you. What's wrong with him? You're gorgeous, intelligent, brilliant in fact, sexy, talented—even my dog loves you. Clearly the guy's a jerk. Tell me about him. Married, I assume," he guessed, and she nodded, finding it hard to believe she'd been pulled into the conversation. Brandon was a character, talented, a brilliant actor, and definitely outrageous. "Married men always make women cry—their wives, their girlfriends, they're a mess. And if he's married, that tells you he's a cheater. That really makes him questionable. Personally, I don't like cheaters. What's wrong with him?"

"It's complicated. He's afraid to get close to anyone," she said as she bent low to take photographs of Brandon's arms and legs for future reference. Thornton licked her face, and Brandon told him to sit. He did and held out a paw to shake hands.

The Portrait

"Your friend sounds dramatic," he said, frowning, thinking about it. "He'll be back. Drama guys always come back, after they make everyone cry and get hysterical."

"I'm not hysterical, I'm just sad," she said, feeling ridiculous having this conversation with Brandon.

"Let him cry and wail, and moan about getting close. You go out and have some fun, and ignore him. Drama guys always come back. They get bored when no one pays attention to them. You know, you and I could really have some fun. We could wind up in the tabloids together and make him jealous." She was laughing by then.

"But then no one would take me seriously as an artist."

"Movie stars would. They would flock to your doors. But I guess they already do. I had to wait eight months for this sitting," he said seriously. But he had boosted her spirits, and the dog was sweet, even if he was the size of a small horse. He weighed a hundred and eighty pounds, Brandon had told her.

It was the most unusual sitting she'd had, and they had fun talking every day. He told her about skin care, how to get thicker hair, gave her the name of his trainer, and described his exercise routine in minute detail. He brought her some of his vitamins, and the name of his plastic surgeon. He was fifty-two and looked thirty-eight at most. He was a bottomless pool of information about how to look more beautiful, be healthier, do relaxation exercises, and find inner peace. His entire life was dedicated to how he looked and felt. He was fun and funny, while she mourned Charlie, and she didn't believe Brandon that he'd be back. Charlie's wounds were too deep, and it was easier for him to live in a dead marriage than to be close to someone he loved. She didn't expect to hear from him again.

Her last session with Brandon was the day before Christmas Eve and he stunned her by giving her a beautiful diamond bracelet. She was embarrassed to accept it, but he insisted, and gave her a big hug when he left, and said he'd had a wonderful time with her.

"You should have slept with me though," he scolded her before he left. "You'd have totally forgotten the jerk by now." She hadn't forgotten him, but she was feeling better. She hadn't finished Brandon's portrait, but she promised it to him in early January. It was obvious that Charlie wouldn't be coming to have his portrait painted. She was going to wait until the first week in January, and have the gallery return his money to him. She hadn't had the heart to do it yet.

She had no plans for Christmas, which she knew would be hard. It always was. She was going to work through the holidays, and she would forget what day it was, which always happened when she was working. She wondered if Brandon Yates was right and she should have more fun. He said she took life too seriously. He had told her that she had amazing eyes, and a very good nose. She smiled every time she looked at his portrait. It was different and fun, and the props they'd used were working well. He had worn a black turtleneck sweater and black trousers, and with the Gothic effect, it was a very powerful painting, and Thornton added a certain panache to it as well. It was eccentric and humorous, which her paintings usually weren't. They were beautiful and serious. But this one was full of Brandon's personality. And there

The Portrait

was something sexy and smoldering about it too. He posed well. He was a very handsome man.

She wore his diamond bracelet on Christmas Eve, and went to bed early. She followed her grandmother's recipe of a glass of brandy before she went to bed, and woke up early to work on Brandon's painting. She had finished the figure, and only had some minor work to do on the background, and Thornton's collar. She was pleased with the result. It was an upbeat end to a hard year. She was sorry she wouldn't be doing the portrait of Charlie. She tried to force herself not to think of him. She was going to have time off in January, since she had set the whole month aside for him. She thought about trying some of Brandon's beauty routines, which was unlike her, but she had nothing else to do.

She finished Brandon's portrait on Christmas Day. Her phone rang once from a blocked number. She reached over to answer it, and it had disconnected. It was probably a wrong number. She had harbored a last hope that Charlie would relent and call her for Christmas, but he hadn't. She went to bed that night, thinking about him, and she looked at the photograph of Axel she kept next to her bed. "*Joyeux Noël*," she whispered, and kissed it, and lay in bed for a long time thinking of the people she loved who had come and gone in her life. And now Charlie was added to the list.

Liam had come home for Christmas as he promised, and looked healthy and well. He was spending almost all of his time outdoors, except what he spent at the drawing board, working on the design for his project. Charlie was happy to see him, and Liam got busy with his friends right away. When Charlie asked, he said his ankle still ached from time to time in damp weather, of which there was a lot in Normandy, but it had healed well and felt strong again. And he was still dating the same girl.

Faye had done what she always did on holidays. She had called a caterer, and they had a sumptuous meal on Christmas Day. They had caviar and local crab, which they loved, and pasta with a delicate truffle sauce, and chocolate soufflé and a Yule log for dessert. It was a perfect end to the day, which had been uneventful. Their florist had decorated the house for Christmas. There was a silver tree with silver ornaments and tiny sparkling lights in the living room. It didn't have a warm personal touch, but it was very chic, and what Charlie expected of Faye. She had her assistant pick their gifts, which Liam had predicted.

Charlie was relaxing in the living room after dinner, after Liam went out. He had no idea where Faye was. She was leaving for Aspen the next day, and was spending New Year's Eve with her friends there. Charlie was spending it alone, which he didn't mind, and actually preferred. They had exchanged gifts that morning. They gave Liam a Rolex watch, and Charlie had bought Faye new skis and a parka, and she had given him a sweater. Liam had brought his father a warm cashmere scarf from Hermès in Deauville, and a silk scarf for his mother.

Charlie had thought of Devon all day. He had promised himself he would call her by or on Christmas, and he hadn't. He had nothing new to say, and he was sure she didn't want to hear from him

The Portrait

by then. He remembered how upset she had been when he vanished for a week in August. Abandoning her for a month after their wonderful week together over Thanksgiving would have been that much worse.

He was drinking a glass of eggnog with brandy when Faye walked into the room. She looked relaxed, and she came to sit on the couch across from him. It was upholstered in a white bouclé fabric their decorator had picked the year before when they bought new couches for the living room.

"Ready for tomorrow?" he asked her pleasantly.

"Thank you for the new skis and the parka. My skis are all beaten up, I needed them, and I've been too busy to buy them." He had bought the newest model from the best brand. She was a fabulous skier, so they would get plenty of use. "I know the timing is awful. But I'm going to be away for three weeks, and your secretary says that you're going to New York, so I don't know when we'll see each other, and there's never a good time," she said as an introduction.

"For what?" It was usually something like a new roof at an outrageous price. Or a new decorator.

"For what I have to say. I've been doing a lot of thinking. I'm five years older than you are, and I'm beginning to think about how I want to spend the last years of my career. The pandemic opened my eyes. I want to work remotely. I'm trapped in my office twelve or fourteen hours a day. I want to work remotely now, and see how it works."

"It won't make much difference from your office, if you're trapped in the house," he said practically.

"From Aspen. Liam's in France. You travel all the time. We never see each other. I'm happy there." He thought about it, and it made sense for her. They would hardly see each other now, maybe every few months, since he got altitude sickness in Aspen. He sometimes wondered if that was why she had picked it.

"If you're happy there, Faye. Why not?" He smiled at her.

"And I want a divorce," she said, and he stared at her.

"Are you serious?" She nodded. "Now? Why?"

"Because the way we live is insane. It's bad for both of us. We have no life except our work. I want to ski every day before I go to work, and maybe lighten up a little. I want to be with people I like, and have a life. Charlie, we don't even know each other anymore. This hasn't made sense for years, except to hide our heads in the sand about how bad our marriage is. We don't even have a marriage. The finances will be complicated, but we're both reasonable, civilized people, we can work it out. There's no reason for us to be married anymore, and Liam is no longer an excuse. I think we should sell this house, unless you want to be here on your own, or you plan to remarry or whatever. I don't need a house this size, nor want one." She had thought it all out carefully. And she looked sure of what she was doing.

"Do you want to remarry?" Charlie looked shocked. He hadn't expected it, and certainly not on Christmas. She had a remarkable way of doing things with total disregard for anyone's emotions except her own. He wasn't upset or hurt, but he was surprised, shocked actually.

"I don't know," she answered his question. "Maybe. Maybe not. If I meet someone, maybe I'd be open to it. But not an empty shell

The Portrait

of a marriage like this one. I don't know how we lasted this long. I think it's been pure laziness on both our parts for the last ten years. You can buy out my half of the house if you want. I want to get something smaller for when I come to work here, or meet with clients. Liam can visit me in Aspen if he wants to see me."

"Have you told him?" Charlie asked her.

"No. You can if you want to." She always left him the dirty work. "I don't think he'll be too upset. The idea of it maybe, but the reality won't be any different from the way we live now." She had really surprised him. He had assumed they'd be married forever. It was what he had told Devon, that his marital status was never going to change. Now everything would be different, but he would be a free man, which was a huge change.

Faye stood up then. She had said her piece, and she was done. There was no sentiment to it, just simple facts.

"I'm sorry to tell you on Christmas. But I wanted to tell you before I left. I don't want to keep it a secret. I don't think anyone we know will be surprised."

"I'm surprised," he said honestly, "but I think it's the right thing to do, if we don't mind the financial upheaval. That will take a while to sort out."

"There's no rush. We have good lawyers and accountants. They'll figure it out," she said calmly. Her announcement had been completely bloodless. There was no emotion to it, and no regret, just a feeling of relief. He felt it too. He had nothing to add. She had covered all the bases, in her usual thorough way, and as unemotionally as always. He wondered if Liam would be upset, or relieved too, after their conversation last summer in East Hampton, about his parents' marriage. Charlie had been honest with him.

Charlie sat alone in the living room, thinking of what Faye had said about selling the house. He thought he'd like a smaller house too. He didn't need a house this size if he was going to be alone now. His mind went immediately to Devon, and what it would change for them. His marriage hadn't really been an issue between them, given the arrangement he and Faye had. The issue for him was the death of his mother and how badly it had marked him. He would no longer have the excuse of being married with women he dated. He would be fair game now, which he wasn't looking forward to. There was no woman he wanted except Devon, and he wasn't up to being with her either. He had managed to be married to Faye for twenty-three years without ever being attached to her or in love with her. He realized that it was an abysmal statement about him that he had tolerated an empty marriage, and he knew he wouldn't miss Faye. He wasn't even sad about the divorce.

He put his empty glass in the kitchen, and went to his room. He was thinking about Devon, not Faye. He wanted to call her and tell her about the divorce. He called her from the landline in his room, wondering what to say after a month of silence. He was longing to hear her voice, her smooth, soothing, comforting voice. And then he thought about what he'd done to her, after their week together. He had walked out on her again and abandoned her and hurt her again. He was no different now. The only thing different was that he wouldn't be married. It wouldn't change all the rest. The phone rang three times at her end, and he hung up before she answered. He didn't have the heart to call her and say—what? Merry Christ-

The Portrait

mas? Sorry you're alone? Guess what, I'm getting divorced? He felt like a complete heel calling her now. She was better off without him and his open wounds. Hers were far deeper than his, and more recent, and he had hurt her again by cutting off all communication. He felt like a complete sonofabitch. He didn't deserve her.

He didn't feel crazy or panicked anymore. He had calmed down. He just felt sad. He had walked out on the best woman he'd ever known. She didn't deserve this. The best thing he could do for her now was leave her alone to get over him in peace. He loved her enough to do that, as his final gift to her.

Faye had already left for Aspen by the time Liam got up the day after Christmas. Charlie was hanging around the house waiting for him when he finally made it to the kitchen, looking slightly hung over, which was reasonable at twenty-two, home for the holidays and out with his friends.

"Did Mom leave?" he asked his father with a yawn, as he poured some milk into a bowl of cereal, and sat down with it, and a cup of coffee.

"Can I make you some eggs?" Charlie offered, and Liam grinned at him sheepishly.

"No, I'm fine. Thanks anyway."

"Yes, your mom left at the crack of dawn to catch the early flight."

"Did she say when she's coming back?" he asked. "I'm going back to Paris in a week."

"She's going to be in Aspen for a while. She wants to try working remotely. She's happy there."

"That's interesting. Everyone else is going back to their offices." Charlie decided that he couldn't put it off any longer, so he dove in.

"We're getting divorced," he said, in one gulp, and waited for what Liam would say. He looked at his father long and hard.

"Are you serious?"

"I am. It was your mom's idea, but I think she's right. I didn't have the guts to do it. She did. It's long overdue. She says she wants to have a life, and she's right. We've been living in the deep freeze for decades. It hasn't made sense in years." Liam's face broke into a broad smile.

"Congratulations!" he said. "Now you get to have a life too. Are you going to start dating?"

"Eventually. I haven't lined up any candidates yet. She told me last night."

"Leave it to Mom to do it on Christmas," Liam said with a chuckle. "She's never great on timing."

"No, she's not. She wanted to get it off her chest before she left. I'm glad she did. Now we can move forward. She wants to sell the house and I agree with her. It's way too big for either of us alone."

"Are you going to get another house?" Liam asked, concerned.

"Yes, a smaller one. Hopefully somewhere around here."

"Can I have a room?"

"Of course. It'll be your home too, for whenever you're here." Liam looked reassured when he said it.

"This is kind of exciting," Liam said. He had wanted them to get divorced for years, they were so miserable together. They were

The Portrait

nothing, not even a couple. It was much harder to explain to his friends growing up than divorced parents would have been. "Can we still have a pool?"

"I'll try. It depends what's available, I haven't started looking. She just told me fourteen hours ago. I'll start looking next week."

Liam went upstairs to get dressed, and Charlie called Adam Stein. He saw Charlie's name on his caller ID.

"Did you call her?" he asked, sounding excited. He assumed that was why Charlie was calling him, to tell him he had talked to Devon.

"No, I didn't. I think I've regained my sanity. After walking out on her for a month, and not answering her texts and calls, I figure she's earned the right to some peace and to forget me. I did a rotten thing to her, twice. She doesn't need any more grief from me. I haven't heard from her for three weeks."

"You're a coward, Charlie Taylor. And you let her go through Christmas alone. You are a total asshole," he said, and meant it.

"I plead guilty on that," Charlie said quietly. He wasn't proud of what he'd done. He'd panicked.

"You could at least call her and tell her you're getting divorced," he said after Charlie told him.

"It's irrelevant. That wasn't the problem."

"It might make a difference to her. It's not a small thing."

"I still left her on her own for the last month, after she spoiled me rotten for a week in New York." Adam hated to hear Charlie give up. But he could hear it in his voice. He sounded defeated about the relationship with Devon, but relieved about the divorce. He asked Adam to get the ball rolling after the holidays.

"Well, congrats on that. For ending the longest dead marriage in the history of the world. You're a free man, or going to be." Charlie felt lighter than he had in years. But there was a rock in his heart at the same time. He had lost Devon. For good this time. It had to be.

Chapter 12

After Devon finished Brandon Yates's portrait on Christmas Day, she decided she loved it. It was a little crazy and eccentric, as he was, but it was so him. Even Thornton's collar looked great, with silver spikes on it that balanced the helmet and the miniature armor. And the dog's expression was perfect. She smiled as she signed it. A castle in a misty forest showed dimly in the background, adding even more fantasy to the painting, which was what Brandon had said he wanted. She had never done a portrait quite like it. It always thrilled her when she did something completely different. It would look great in one of her shows, if he loaned it to her. He had said he would. It really did look medieval, and "Gothic," which had been Brandon's vision.

She had paints all over her palette, and she wanted to clean her brushes. She had bought new supplies the week before Christmas, and a new cleaning fluid for her brushes that the salesclerk at the art supply said was fantastic and would take the paint off a car, which sounded a little extreme, but she agreed to try it. It came in a big bottle, and he told her to wear rubber gloves when she used it. She opened the bottle, and then remembered to get the rubber gloves from under the kitchen sink. She walked into the kitchen holding the bottle with one hand, tripped on the carpet as she approached the sink, and the chemical in the bottle splashed up toward her face and went straight into her eyes. She felt as though someone had put a hatchet through each of her eyes, and everything went instantly black, as she closed them. But it was too late, her eyes were bathed in the toxic chemical, and burned like fire. She dropped the bottle in the sink, groping her way to find it, and the solution got on her hands too. Her eyes and her hands were burning, and when she opened her eyes, she could see light and dark, but no shapes. She was temporarily blinded by the product. She tried to find her way around her kitchen and was bumping into things, with the excruciating pain in her eyes. She thought of calling her downstairs neighbor, and remembered that he was in Florida for the holidays, visiting his mother. She had no one to call and she couldn't see, and the pain was almost unbearable. She didn't know what else to do and she couldn't stand the pain. She groped her way back to the studio, trying to remember where she had left her phone. She thought it was on the table with her paints. And every time she tried to open her eyes to find her way, all she could see by then was darkness, and no light at all.

She was crying from the pain when she finally found her phone in her purse and called 911. They answered immediately.

"I'm blind," she said to the operator. "I spilled a chemical in my eyes and I can't see, and the pain is terrible." She was sobbing.

The Portrait

"Do you know what the chemical was?"

"No, I don't. I'm an artist, and I'm blind. Can you send someone to help me? I have to go to a hospital." The operator checked with dispatch.

"They'll be with you in ten minutes. Is your building locked?"

"Yes."

"Can you open your front door? We'll have the police get us into the building," she said. Devon almost fainted from the pain as she groped her way to the door, and collapsed after she unlocked it. She left it open—there was no one in the building, which was divided into two apartments, and her neighbor was gone. She drifted in and out of consciousness as she waited, crouched on the floor, and she heard sirens in the distance and wondered if they were for her. A few minutes later she heard the outer door being forced, and heavy footsteps running up the stairs. She called out so they could find her. All she could see by then was blackness, and a male voice told her they were going to lay her down on a gurney.

"What's your name?" the voice asked her.

"Devon Darcy," she said in a voice contorted with the excruciating pain in her eyes, and her arms and hands were burning too, they felt like they were on fire.

"I'm Mike, I'm a paramedic, and Ellen and Jake are here with me," the voice said. "I'm going to flush your eyes with a sterile saline solution. We're going to do that all the way to the hospital. Can you open your eyes for me?" His voice was strong and firm.

"I don't know, they burn so much." She was crying and felt nauseous and dizzy from the pain, as she felt a gentle hand take hers and hold it while they poured the saline solution in her eyes and on her hands and arms, and then she was lifted onto the gurney, covered with a blanket, and strapped in.

"We're going to leave fast now. Do you have any of the chemical left that burned you?" Mike asked.

"I dropped the bottle in the kitchen sink," she said, as Jake covered her with another blanket and Ellen went to find the bottle, and Mike kept flushing her eyes with a steady stream of the saline solution.

"I left my purse in the kitchen, my phone is in it," she said. She was shaking from the pain and in shock.

Ellen was back a minute later. "Got it," she said to Mike. "There's about a third of the bottle left," she said hastily and told Devon she had her purse and phone.

"We're out of here," Mike said telling Jake to turn out the lights and asking Ellen to get Devon's keys out of her purse to lock the door, and a minute later Devon heard the door close and she felt them tip the gurney to get her down the stairs, while Ellen continued the steady stream of saline solution to her eyes. Devon's face and neck were soaked by the solution, and her eyes never stopped burning for a second, nor did her hands and arms. They were on fire, and she couldn't see anything, only blackness.

Devon felt them set the gurney down in the ambulance and heard the doors slam. She was still in terrible pain and heard the siren as they raced to the hospital. They rushed her into the trauma unit, and everything was moving quickly. They were still flushing her eyes with the saline solution and had washed her hands and arms to get the chemicals off them, to stop them from burning her further. Different voices of people she couldn't see kept asking her

The Portrait

questions. She was then rushed to the operating room, where they put her under anesthesia to clean her eyes and treat her burns.

Devon had an overwhelming sense of panic and no one to call. She was alone, wondering if she would ever see again. When she woke up, she was in the recovery room, and when she was fully awake, a doctor came to see her. A soft tube had been placed in each eye connected to a sterile saline solution, like an IV, to continue flushing her eyes. The doctor explained that the flushing would continue for twenty-four hours until the pH of her eyes had returned to normal, once all of the chemicals had been washed away. They had put anesthetic drops in her eyes while she was unconscious, so she was momentarily out of pain.

Dr. Allen, the head of ophthalmology, explained to her that the solution that had gotten into her eyes contained sodium hydroxide, lye in layman's terms, common in industrial cleaning solutions, ammonia, and calcium hydroxide, which had resulted in a grade III alkali burn to her eyes. He said that damage to the cornea occurs within one to five minutes, and can happen within fifteen seconds of the injury, and the paramedics arriving on the scene quickly had been vital for her long-term recovery. They would monitor the pressure inside her eyeballs, and antibiotic ointments and steroids would be used to prevent infection. He said it would take several weeks to assess the extent of the injury, and determine whether it had caused permanent damage to her eyes. They were guardedly hopeful, but they could not yet rule out blindness or the loss of her eyes as a result. But they hoped that would not be the case. And she would have to remain in the hospital to be properly monitored and have the ointments applied every few hours, and he assured her that he and the senior resident, Dr. Louise Lovato, would be treating her themselves.

Devon listened to Dr. Allen in a haze, and the words that kept sending shockwaves through her were "blind," and the loss of her sight, and even her eyes. It was a huge price to pay for a stumble in her kitchen with a bottle of cleaning solution in her hand. She couldn't imagine her life if she went blind. After the doctor spoke to her, the nurse gave her a shot to sedate her and make her sleep, and they moved her to a private room. Before the nurse gave her the shot, she gently asked Devon if there was anyone she wanted to call, and she shook her head. She had no one to call, and there was no point calling Charlie. If he didn't want her when she was healthy and whole, he wouldn't want her blind, and she was too proud to call him. She drifted into a drugged sleep after the shot, her tears mixing with the saline solution flushing her eyes.

When Devon woke in the morning, she was still in pain. She was alone in the room, and she could hear noises and voices in the distance. Dr. Allen returned as she was waking up, and she remembered him. He introduced her to Dr. Lovato, who sounded young and sympathetic.

Dr. Allen was as kind and cautious about the outcome as he had been the night before. She was still hooked up to the flushing mechanism and she felt as though she had knives in her eyes.

Dr. Allen told her they had placed a call to the manufacturer of the cleaning solution to learn more about it, and by that afternoon they were going to start the antibiotic and steroid ointments and would be putting sterile pads on her eyes. He asked her again if there was any family member or friend she wanted them to call.

The Portrait

"Is there anyone you'd like us to call to come and be with you?" There had been no next of kin listed on any of the papers in her purse. She had no "kin" to list.

"No, there isn't." She was fighting back tears while talking to them. She thought of Charlie again but there was no way she was going to call him now, in the situation she was in, blind and injured, when he wouldn't speak to her when she was well. He had abandoned her, and she had to manage now on her own. It was a frightening situation, and she had no idea if she would ever see again. There were chemical burns on her face and hands as well, but they were responding to the ointments on them.

"We feel confident that the skin burns will heal. We had a plastic surgeon look at them last night in the O.R.," the female voice of Dr. Lovato told her. "What we don't know enough about yet are your eyes. It's going to take some time to assess the damage." She echoed Dr. Allen. "We're hoping there won't be long-term consequences from the accident."

"I'm an artist," Devon said in a hoarse voice. She had been saying it since she arrived, as though that fact could save her from blindness.

"Do you have family in the area, or a close friend?" Dr. Lovato asked her. She exchanged a look with Dr. Allen. They were both deeply affected by Devon's situation. And with grade III alkali burns to her eyes, the outcome was uncertain.

"No, I don't," Devon confirmed. She had friends, but no one she was close enough to want to burden them with her being blind in a hospital. And then she thought of her gallery. She didn't even know what day it was, or if the gallery was open. She thought it was two days after Christmas, but she had lost track of time. "What day is it?" she asked them.

"It's Monday," Dr. Lovato said gently.

"The gallery is closed on Mondays, but there should be someone there. If you could call the Kingsley Stone Gallery on Madison Avenue, and ask for Edward Stone, and tell him I'm here. Did they bring my phone with me?" Devon couldn't remember and felt helpless. A nurse had brought her a bedpan when she woke up. She couldn't even get to the bathroom on her own.

"I'll check," Dr. Lovato reassured her. "The paramedics brought your purse. I'll look for your phone." Devon heard a cupboard open, and the young woman came back to Devon quickly, and handed it to Devon. She couldn't see to make calls, but at least she could receive them, if the gallery wanted to reach her. "I'll call the gallery as soon as I get back to the desk."

"What time is it?" Devon asked her in a shaking voice. She felt suffocated by the darkness she was in. It felt claustrophobic and made her feel panicked. Between the darkness and the pain, she felt lost and disoriented, and the anesthesia the night before and the shot for the pain exacerbated the feeling.

"It's ten-thirty in the morning," Dr. Allen told her.

"There should be someone at the gallery by now. If you could have Edward Stone call me, I'd appreciate it."

"I know this is frightening, but you'll get oriented soon," Dr. Lovato said. "We'll have the nurses check you every ten minutes or so," and she put a call button in Devon's hand. "And we're hoping that in the coming weeks the effects of the chemicals will start to lessen and your vision will improve. I know this isn't easy. We're going to do everything we can to reverse the effects of the chemicals." She had a kind voice, and she held Devon's hand while she spoke to her, which was comforting. Devon had never felt so lost and helpless in her life. She couldn't feed herself, or get to the bathroom. She couldn't see anything. She was in total darkness. She saw nothing with her eyes open, not even the smallest hint of light. "I'm going to be back to check you in a little while," Dr. Lovato said.

"And I'm going to see you twice a day," Dr. Allen said in a more cheerful tone.

"You have our full attention," Dr. Lovato said. "I'll call Edward Stone now, and have him call you. I'll let you know if I reach him."

"If he's not there, someone at the gallery will call him, if you tell them it's for Devon Darcy and that it's an emergency."

"I promise I will," Dr. Lovato said, and the two doctors left her a minute later, as Devon lay in her bed shaking with the shock and anxiety of what had happened. She was overwhelmed by panic. She lay there trying to stay calm, and Dr. Lovato came back five minutes later.

"They said they were going to call Mr. Stone at home immediately. I told them where you are and what happened."

"Thank you," Devon said, and wiped the tears from her cheeks. She couldn't stop crying, she was so frightened. And her eyes were tearing and swollen.

The cell phone rang five minutes later. Edward Stone was one of the two owners of her gallery. She was closer to Edward than to Tom Kingsley, who was older and more serious. Edward had been her champion at the gallery since she'd been there.

She answered the phone, and her voice sounded like a croak from the anesthetic the night before.

"Devon?" He sounded as panicked as she felt. "What happened?" She told him, and he sounded distraught.

"It was so stupid, I tripped, and the chemical just flew out of the bottle and up into my face. Edward, I can't see anything. I'm totally blind." She started sobbing as soon as she said the words. There was no worse possible fate for her. It was like a death sentence.

"I called the trauma unit, and spoke to the chief resident. She said they're hoping for some rapid improvement in the next two weeks." It seemed a long time to wait, to both of them. "Don't panic. Is there anyone with you?" He knew how solitary she was and how hard she worked. She had no family, and only a few friends.

"No," she said, her voice still shaking.

"I'm going to come down there right away and organize things for you. You need a nurse with you around the clock until your eyes clear." He was ready to jump in and help.

"Thank you, Edward. I'm sorry to be such a nuisance. It was so stupid of me. I finished the Brandon Yates painting and I wanted to clean my brushes. The painting is gorgeous. It's a little crazy, but it's exactly what he wanted. I even got his dog in. He loves it."

"Brandon Yates is a little crazy. I can't wait to see it." It suddenly dawned on her that it might be the last portrait she ever painted, and she felt panicked again.

"They said I would be here for weeks. I don't even know where I am."

"You're at NYU hospital. They have some of the best doctors in the city. And I'm going to check everyone out. Don't worry. Do you need anything?"

"No. I'm fine. Thank you for taking care of everything." Her voice shook as she started to cry again. He was crying too, but she couldn't hear it. He was trying to sound upbeat for her. But he was as panicked as she was. He had been horrified when he got the call from the gallery, and they told him what had happened.

He was at the hospital half an hour later, and marched into the room in his usual take-charge way. He was the life force of the gallery, and he treated all their artists like his children, and Devon was his favorite. He came over to her bed and gently stroked her hair. There were marks on her face where the chemical had splashed her, and dressings, and her eyes were red and swollen. He helped her get her bed in a sitting position. She said she felt dizzy and sick. He felt sick seeing her too, but his voice gave away none of what he felt, nor his terror that she would remain blind from the accident. Dr. Lovato had acknowledged to him that it was a worst-case possibility.

"I've arranged for nurses twenty-four hours a day. The first shift will be here at noon." She would have to be fed and bathed and taken to the bathroom. She was totally helpless without being able to see. "Did you bring any clothes with you?" he asked her. She was wearing a hospital gown. She wasn't sick, she was injured and blind, and she could feel that she had bandages on her hands and arms with topical ointments, since all traces of the chemicals had been removed.

"I didn't pack," she said with a small smile. "I was wearing a sweatshirt and jeans, I don't know where they went." He opened the narrow cupboard, and saw the jeans folded on the floor of the closet. The sweatshirt was soaked with chemicals and had been discarded.

"They're here," he reassured her. "If you give me your keys, I'll go to the apartment and pack a bag for you."

"I'm sorry to bother you with that. Why don't you have one of the girls from the gallery do it?"

"I'm happy to do whatever I can for you," he said gently, and came to sit down in the chair next to her.

"I have a booking in January we need to cancel," she told him. "It's the only one in January, a Charles Taylor from San Francisco. We need to send his money back. I don't know if he paid a deposit or in full. Just tell him it's canceled, don't reschedule, and don't tell him that I'm injured or here."

"Do you know him? I think he paid in full."

"I was going to cancel it anyway, and yes, I do know him. I don't think he would have been happy with the portrait. He had something different in mind," she said vaguely. She didn't want Charlie to find out what had happened to her, and to come back out of pity. He had closed the door on her firmly, and she wasn't going to open it, or play the sympathy card. She didn't want to appear pathetic. Charlie was out of her life for good.

Edward spoke to her calmly. He could see how upset she was, which was understandable. He was just praying that the chemicals wouldn't have lasting effects. People had been blinded by less, and in her case it would be a tragedy, and she didn't deserve to have this happen to her. She was the sweetest person he knew, and he

The Portrait

was well aware of her personal history. This was one blow too many. It would be an unbearable end to the story.

Edward stayed for an hour and he found her keys in her purse. He said he'd have her bag dropped off later by his driver. Her nurse could get her organized. And she reminded him before he left to look at Brandon's portrait when he went to her apartment.

He called her from her place when he got there.

"Oh my God, Devon, it's fantastic. It's a total fantasy."

"It was his fantasy, and I was nervous about it at first, but I went with it, and we both love the result. Even the dog looks fabulous."

"Where did you get the miniature armor, or did you just make that up?"

"No, I brought it from Paris."

"It's the perfect little twist and eye-catcher, to balance the composition." There was always some special little object or quirk in Devon's paintings, something that was meaningful to the subject or to her, that added her special touch to the painting. Edward had cried when he saw it, fearing it could be her last. He couldn't bear to think it, and he refused to believe it. He had called Dr. Allen on the way to the apartment, and the doctor also had said that there was the possibility that she could remain blind, but they had no way of knowing yet, and he was hoping that wouldn't happen. With a grade III alkali injury it was also possible she would recover her sight. Edward had told the doctor that she was one of the most important contemporary portrait artists in the country, possibly the world, and they had to do everything humanly possible to save her sight, and the doctor had assured Edward they would. They already were, with the ongoing flushing and the ointments they were planning to start that night. The most important thing was that she had gotten there quickly after the injury, and the paramedics had flushed her eyes vigorously. What remained to be seen was how much damage the chemicals had done and if it could be reversed or not.

The nurse Edward had hired from a private registry was a pleasant upbeat Irishwoman, who helped Devon take a shower, brushed her hair for her, and helped her get dressed. She tucked Devon's arm into hers and got her to walk down the hall to get some exercise. Edward had sent Devon's laptop along with her clothes and an iPad, and the nurse put some music on for her, and got Devon to take a nap. She had been through an enormous trauma, and she needed to calm down and rest. She was still taking strong pain medicine, which wore her out too. She had been through a lot in the past twenty-four hours. And her private nurse on the second shift was just as nice. She was from Martinique, so Devon spoke to her in French, which was comforting too, and reminded her of her grandmother and Jean-Louis. She dreamed of him while she was sleeping, and had woken up in tears. She had told him she was blind and Axel was in the dream too.

Dr. Allen came back to see her that evening, and Dr. Lovato had checked on her before she left. They were extremely attentive. Edward had seen to it that everyone knew she was to get VIP treatment, and the best medical care possible. Edward came back to see her that night himself to make sure that everything was going smoothly. And everyone at the gallery had sent her their love. Tom Kingsley had called her to wish her well. The troops were rallying around her but nothing had changed with her eyes.

The Portrait

She was still engulfed in total darkness, but with so many people being kind to her, she felt less panicked than she had at first. But she was still in a great deal of pain.

Charlie had contacted a realtor that day, the same one he had used to list his father's house, which was currently in escrow. He listed the house in Atherton, and told the realtor he was looking for a smaller house in the same area, suitable for him and his son. He wanted comfort and space, without being as vast as the house he was selling, and a pool if possible, he said, remembering Liam's request.

He had a busy day starting to get the divorce rolling, and listing the house. And at the end of it, he sat quietly in the library he used as an office at home. He missed Devon unbearably and wanted to tell her he was getting divorced. He took out his cell phone and stared at it for a long time, and finally called her number. She was likely asleep when he called and it went to voicemail. Or she had opted not to take his call. He couldn't blame her. It had been just over a month since he'd seen her and never contacted her again, and ignored all her calls and messages. He assumed that her not taking his call was her final message to him to leave her alone.

When he got his check from the gallery by FedEx the next day, with a formal letter, it had the ring of finality to it. The Kingsley Stone Gallery informed him that the artist had canceled his commission, feeling that the portrait requested would not be a successful collaboration, and thought it wisest not to proceed, hence the return of his payment in full. The letter was signed by Edward

Stone. Charlie wasn't surprised but it hurt anyway. It was all the consequence of his shabby treatment of her, which he fully recognized. Her not taking his call, canceling the portrait, and returning his check said it all. She had severed any connection to him. He had been afraid of losing her if he became too attached to her, but he was attached to her anyway, and had lost her just as surely. He felt the same agonizing tearing of his soul that she had been feeling for the past month. Until then, he had had the option to reach out to her if he was brave enough. Now he knew that door had closed, and she wouldn't open it to him again. It was a searing pain and felt like a death.

When Devon woke up, after taking her painkillers, her nurse told her there had been a missed call while she was sleeping and read the number to her. Devon recognized it as Charlie's number immediately. She thought of returning the call. But what could she say to him? That she was blind now and might never see again and her career might be over? That she still loved him, but refused to be a burden to him? Or that she was terrified and in pain and he had broken her heart? There was nothing she could say that didn't sound pathetic, so she said nothing, just as he had, and didn't return the call. It really was over now, and had to be forever. There was no turning back from the path he had set them on. If he had continued their relationship after Thanksgiving, she would have dreaded being a burden to him, but he would have been there and they would have faced it together. But now she had to face the fact that he didn't want her, he had abandoned her, whatever the reason, she was alone, and he was out of her life forever. And if she was going to be blind, she thought that maybe it was just as well that he had been spared.

They removed the flushing device that night and began the application of antibiotic and steroid ointments into her eyes, repeating the treatment at frequent intervals. After a week, there was the first slight sign of improvement, as she could see light and dark now. She couldn't see shapes, just as it had happened right after the accident, but she could see light. It was the first hopeful sign since the accident, and she cried when the first glimmers of light and shadows appeared. And Edward cried when she called the gallery and told him. He had come every day. Brandon Yates's painting was dry and had been delivered by then, and he was ecstatic. They didn't tell him what had happened to her. They didn't want anyone to know or for the art world to get wind of it. Devon's blindness was being kept a carefully guarded secret except to the gallery owners and staff, and they had kept it out of the press and social media.

For the next month, Devon's world became as small and dark as her vision, trying new medicines, following new protocols, having consultations. Dr. Allen tried an experimental treatment for a few days, but Devon was allergic to it, so they returned to the original protocols. The doctors had a conference call with the product's manufacturer, who admitted that permanent blindness could occur from an accident like Devon's, with direct contact. No one knew for certain if the toxic effects of the chemicals could be reversed. It was impossible to know which would be true for Devon—restoration of her sight, or blindness, or severely impaired vision. All they could do was to continue her treatment of antibiotics and steroids and hope for the best.

Devon had days of dark depression, and moments of hope. There were weeks of treatment with only slight improvement, and the occasional breakthrough that led everyone on her team to hope and pray that she would see again one day, and even paint. There was no way to say which way it would go. She had gotten very adept at getting around her hospital room without assistance. She could even get around the hospital with one of her nurses, but for now, she was still blind, and the little glimmers of light that she saw were very small. And with each passing week, hope of her recovery was waning.

The treatments she had to endure were painful, but she was very brave. They anesthetized her eyes at times to measure the pressure to see how affected her corneas were and to check for glaucoma. Surgery was a possibility if the treatments didn't work, but there was no guarantee that surgery would be effective, if she remained totally blind. She sat at the window, listening to the street noises and trying to identify what they were. She noticed that her hearing had become more acute, and found that she could hear voices from a great distance and discern what they were saying. She recognized each of the nurses' footsteps, and knew who they were before they spoke. All of her senses were heightened, and she lay in bed at night, wide-awake, overwhelmed by anxiety

The Portrait

and fear for her future. What was to become of her if she remained fully blind? Who would take care of her, and how would she be able to take care of herself? She knew that others did it, but how would she live without being able to paint? She had visions in her mind of things she had seen and still wanted to paint. She would rather have lost a limb than her eyes. She could have painted from a wheelchair, but there was nothing she could do without her sight. She had lost so many people she loved in the course of her lifetime, and now she had lost herself.

A psychiatrist came to see her every few days, and there was talk of eventually moving her to a rehabilitation center for the sight-impaired, if there was no improvement. Once they moved her there, she knew they would have given up on her and expected her to adjust to her situation. She didn't want to adjust to it, she wanted to fight and do everything she could to get her sight back. But by the end of January, she was sinking into a deep depression, and she was losing hope. Nothing had changed.

Chapter 13

After Faye's decision, announced to him at Christmas, Charlie's life was leaping ahead. After years of not dealing with their situation, his whole life revolved around those changes now. It felt like a free fall at times, but he was handling as much of it as he could. He put the house in Atherton on the market at the beginning of January, and there were open houses every weekend. Only qualified buyers were invited, and the most important realtors. At the same time, Charlie was looking for a smaller house for himself and Liam, whenever he would be home. Despite all the details he had to attend to, there was something invigorating about the process. He felt as though he were being swept on the tides to better times. With each day, he realized that they should have done this years before. Dealing with it now was like clearing away the deadwood in his life, getting rid of the old, and finding a new place to live. The big house made no sense anymore, and like everything else in their marriage, had made no sense for years.

He wanted to stay in the same area, with grounds similar to what they'd had, and he didn't want to undertake years of remodeling. He wanted to find a house he could move into now, and transition quickly. By the time Liam came home for another visit, Charlie wanted to be settled in their new home, to give him a sense of continuity.

Charlie reported to Faye on any progress and consulted her on decisions that affected them both, since they were joint owners of their current property, but she seemed happy to let him handle all the details and do the heavy lifting, which was nothing new. She was used to delegating, and she was more than happy to do that from a distance, and let Charlie do all the work.

There was a lot of interest at the first open house, and two offers after the second one, both of which were lowballs, which were of no interest. Charlie knew both prospective buyers and that they could go considerably higher and were just trying to take advantage of the circumstances, but he and Faye were a united front on that. They wanted top dollar for their beautiful home, even if it meant waiting for a while for the right buyer to show up. He was sure there was one, especially with all the young tech families in the area.

In the last week of January, after three open houses, and ads in all the best decorating and architectural magazines, thanks to their realtor, a young family came to see it for the second time. They had four children and the husband had just sold a very successful startup, and had money he had no idea what to do with. The house he purchased was going to be their first important home. They went over every inch of the house, and brought an architect with them, which the realtor said was a good sign. Char-

The Portrait

lie was in the house, in his home office, in case they had any questions, but he didn't interfere.

The couple wanted to know if he would be interested in a fast all-cash closing, and he said he wasn't adverse to it, if he found the right home for himself, and he would have to discuss any offers with his ex-wife as well. Unlike many divorces, Faye and Charlie were on good terms and agreed on what they wanted for the house. It was a lot of money, but they had no pressing need financially. Unlike many people who were getting divorced, where it became a battle, the Taylors' position was simple and clean.

On the first of February, Charlie's realtor showed him a house that was coming on the market, and not listed yet. It belonged to a venture capitalist in Boston, who owned the house but didn't live there, and had only used it when he came to Silicon Valley to work on deals. He had sold his business and was retiring, and he and his wife were moving to Tuscany and had no use for the house anymore, and their children were grown and scattered everywhere from London to Dubai to New York.

The house looked brand-new when Charlie saw it. There were two wings and a fairly large central body of the house with rooms to entertain, including a big, beautiful living room with high ceilings and skylights that looked out on several acres of natural woodland. There was a large glassed-in dining room with walls that rolled back and opened into the garden. One wing held the master suite and the other two large guest bedrooms. The owner had built a small golf course at the back of the property. There were tennis courts, and a fairly large pool. Everything was state-of-the-art—spa, sauna, a big kitchen with gleaming equipment. The owners had bought the house and hardly used it, and the location was even better than that of Faye and Charlie's current home. Charlie liked the fact that Liam and his friends would be at the opposite end of the house. And there was a barbecue area and patio area where Liam could hang out with his friends, near the pool but far enough from the master suite that they wouldn't disturb Charlie. There was a neatly built shed near the pool with two dressing rooms, a pool table, and a Ping-Pong table. It had everything that Charlie could have wanted. The house was only five years old, so everything was barely used. It was kind of an indoor-outdoor space for good weather with retractable walls, and it was three miles closer to his office than their current home. He was shocked at how reasonable the price was, and was suspicious of it at first.

"Is there something wrong with it that I don't know about?" Charlie asked his realtor. "A train that comes by every hour somewhere on the property, or a poisoned well?" The realtor laughed.

"No, they're just very reasonable people. They don't want to hang onto it for years. They don't need the money, and they want to be free to start their new life in Tuscany, without having to maintain a house here, now that he has sold his business. He wanted to sell it to the people who bought his company as part of the deal, but they love the house they're in, they have five kids, and they don't want to move. The one handicap for most people is that it's really an adult home, with the master suite and only two other bedrooms. Most families in this area want at least four bedrooms, and they're one shy." But it was perfect for Charlie and Liam, at opposite ends of the house. Liam could have a guest stay

The Portrait

when he came home, or Charlie could have guests when Liam was away, which was most of the time now. It was almost too easy.

"What kind of closing do they want?" he asked.

"Whatever you want. They're ready to hand a new buyer the keys. I think a thirty-day closing would be fine, if you're anxious to move."

Charlie smiled at him. "Well, Jack, I need to check it with Faye, but if she's amenable, it looks like the family buying our house could have their thirty-day closing, and everybody gets what they want." The realtor was thrilled with the transaction.

Charlie called Faye as soon as he got home.

"That's fantastic, and I think it's a fair price for ours, don't you?"

"I do." Their house was in perfect shape, and so was his new one. "I don't see the point of haggling for another twenty or thirty thousand dollars. We're getting the right price and I love the one I just saw. What about you when you come back to work here?" he asked her.

"I've thought about it a lot. I want a condo, I don't want a house. I have a house here, and all I do is come home to sleep when I'm in Palo Alto. I don't entertain, and I don't want to deal with high maintenance and headaches. I'll look for something the next time I'm there, and I can rent in the meantime."

"It looks like we have a deal then," and a very respectable amount of money to split in the divorce, and he loved the home he had just seen for himself and Liam.

He called the realtor after he spoke to Faye, and they agreed to the prices on both homes, with thirty-day closings on his sale and the new purchase. It couldn't have been simpler or smoother. "I won't have an excuse for my lousy golf game anymore with six holes on the property to practice with, except that I have no time to practice. You'll have to come over and try it out with me sometime."

"I'd be delighted." It was one of the best days he'd had in years. Both homes had sold easily to the right new owners, people who loved them. And Charlie sent Liam a text, "You've got your pool." He sent him photos of the property by text, and Liam called all excited when he woke and saw them.

"When do we move, Dad?"

"Sometime in early March. We'll be all moved in the next time you come home." It boosted Charlie's spirits immeasurably, and took a little of the sting out of how badly things had ended with Devon. He was still sad about it, but tried not to dwell on it. Adam had stopped asking him, and was sad for Charlie that he hadn't tackled his issues and tried to make it work. Charlie had told him that he had called her a few days after Christmas, that she hadn't returned the call or answered his message, so he left her alone after that. He was sorry about the portrait too. He had told the board at the bank that they would have to live without a portrait of him. He didn't have the heart to do one with anyone else now. The portrait she would have done would have been a beauty, but it was not meant to be. He just told the board that the artist had canceled due to a scheduling conflict, and didn't say why. He was continuing the role he had promised his father to fulfill as chairman of the board, but he was privately planning to resign by the end of the year.

* * *

The Portrait

The winds of change were in the air for Charlie. Two weeks after he found his new home, he got a serious offer from a group in Texas who wanted to buy the startup he had been nurturing and growing for nearly twenty years. It was the first offer he'd had in a range that made it seriously interesting. He put all his advisors and money people on it, and even discussed it with Faye, who was still the smartest woman he knew and one of the best heads in venture capital, and she advised him to take it. The company making the offer was very well-known, solid, and respectable.

"You can't take it much further than you have. You've grown the company as big as it should get, any bigger and it will be unmanageable. You can start something new after you sell. You like taking them from the ground up. You're too young to retire—you need a new game to play. If I were you, I would take the deal and run with the money," she said, and he laughed.

"You give the best advice in the business," he said admiringly.

"Thank you. I'm just a shitty wife. It's not my long suit," but she liked the idea that they could still be friends. It was all they had been for years anyway, with the burden of marriage, and none of the advantages. They were both happier now, as their son had predicted they would be. Liam was a smart guy too. It had been obvious to everyone for years, except them. Charlie was glad she had woken up, even if he hadn't. But he was pleased with the way things were working out, as long as they could talk to each other and stay friends. Not all of their financial arrangements had been worked out, but they were getting there. Adam had suggested that they separate the financial negotiations from the rest so that the divorce could go through, and they wouldn't get stuck, married for several more years while they worked out the last financial details, and they both liked the idea. They were ready to be free. The divorce was going to be final at the end of June.

Devon's February did not go as smoothly as Charlie's. He had no idea where she was or what had happened to her. There had been a brief skirmish with the hospital. They wanted to put her in a rehab center, which was far away on Long Island, with mostly older non-sighted people, but Devon wanted to stay at NYU hospital with her doctors near at hand. Edward Stone wanted her there too, so he could keep a close eye on her and the medical staff around her. Since she was a long-term patient and nowhere near able to go home, the administration at NYU wanted to send her to long-term rehab. Devon had objected, and in the end, the rehab had decided that she still needed too much medical attention, which they did not have the staff at the rehab facility to administer, so she got to stay in her familiar room with the nurses she knew who took such good care of her, and the doctors she liked. Edward was close friends with the head of the hospital board and was a big donor, so she was secure where she was. There was no firm date for her departure from the hospital, which Dr. Allen explained to her was good news. They were still hoping for improvement. Once they discharged her it meant that they had taken her as far in her recovery as she could go. And the doctor was honest with her—it could take several more months. He didn't believe that she was a candidate for surgery, and there were enough minor

The Portrait

improvements to lead him to hope that she could still recover, although he didn't promise it.

She missed being able to go out, and felt cooped up in her room, but they applied ointments and drops, and examined her so many times a day that she was busy all day long, and she chatted with the nurses when they came to check on her. Edward came to visit her almost every day, and treated her like a daughter, and Devon was so grateful for what they were doing for her that she made a large donation to the hospital too. They switched her room then to an enormous corner room on the same floor that was only available to large donors and important politicians like the governor or a senator. The new suite gave her more room to move around. And every day they tested her vision and nothing significant had changed. She could still only see light and dark and nothing more. Her eyes were bandaged most of the time, except when they were checking her, or if they left them off for a while.

There were times that Devon was deeply discouraged. She missed painting desperately, coupled with the fear that she might never paint again. The gallery had postponed her February and March commissions, and had given the subjects dates in the fall, without telling them why. None of them canceled, and they were even more eager to have portraits done by her. Edward had agreed that they would evaluate the situation month by month. He didn't want to reinforce her fear that her career was over by simply canceling commissions. It just made her future subjects even more eager for their portraits.

The manufacturer of the highly toxic solution that had blinded her was being scrupulously cooperative with Devon's doctors and the laboratory in trying to pinpoint the range of effects from the solution and to estimate her chances for recovery. They were hoping to avoid a lawsuit for selling such a dangerous substance without full disclosure of its potential disastrous effects. There were warnings on the bottle, but not enough, and they had taken the stock they had off the market pending relabeling and further information. Devon was becoming an important case study under the protective name of Jane Doe.

Edward had tracked down two ophthalmologists at Mass General, who also taught at the Harvard Medical School, who were consulting on her case digitally, and she was now a case study of interest for them too.

Very simply, it all boiled down to whether or not she would see again. Regaining her sight fully had become her only focus and her full-time job.

She thought of Charlie often in quiet moments, and wondered how he was. She had no way of knowing, but she hoped he was all right and had not disappeared into his shell as a result of his old wounds when he abandoned her. She realized that she was the wrong partner for him because of her own life experience. She was too fragile on the subject of abandonment and loss to be with someone who used abandonment as both a shield and a weapon to protect himself. He had reopened all her old wounds and they were deep, and she suspected that her issues had triggered his. It was a dangerous combination for them both, and better that he had unhooked from her early and moved on. But she was sad about it anyway. They had loved each other passionately for a

The Portrait

minute and she would always remember their time in East Hampton, Labor Day weekend on his sailboat, and their week of Thanksgiving. She cherished the memories and part of her would always love him. She hoped he was happy now, whatever that meant to him.

Brandon Yates had come to the gallery to thank Edward Stone personally for the portrait Devon had done of him. He said it was the jewel of his collection of portraits and by far his favorite. "She even did a beautiful job with my dog," he said, in awe of her talent.

"She'll be happy to hear it," Edward said warmly. "She is very proud of that portrait, and she loved working with you."

"I think she's fantastic. Such an incredible talent, and we had so much fun. I'm actually having an unveiling party at my apartment," Brandon said. "I know she said she never socializes with her subjects, but do you suppose you could convince her to come? I want her to be the guest of honor. I really adore her, more than any of my leading ladies," Brandon said seriously, "and she wouldn't go out with me." Edward laughed at that. And he was sure that Brandon had tried hard. He was very persistent and very sexy, according to the tabloids. He had few costars he hadn't slept with.

"Devon is a very serious artist, and she has strict boundaries. And although I know she'll be very touched by your invitation, I'm certain, Brandon, that she won't come. She's working very hard on something at the moment." Brandon looked crestfallen when Edward said it, and he had no sooner spoken than his assistant poked her head in the door, and spoke a message to him, since he hadn't picked up the phone when she buzzed him on the intercom.

"Devon's doctor is on the line from the hospital, and he wants to talk to you," she said, and Brandon looked like he'd been shot.

"The hospital? Devon is in the hospital? What happened?" He went pale, and Edward didn't want to lose the doctor's call and decided to do damage control later with Brandon. He picked up the phone with a serious expression. It was about extending her stay, and moving her to the Governor's Suite, so called because three New York governors had stayed there. And it was obvious from Edward's side of the conversation that whatever Devon had was serious, and she was going to be in the hospital for a long time for "treatments." Brandon had been pacing in the room while he listened, and he looked frantic by the time Edward ended the call.

"Oh my God," Brandon said with a look of panic. "Please don't tell me she has cancer. She's the love of my life."

"No, she doesn't. And she's the love of my life too. She's like a daughter to me. She had an accident," Edward said cautiously.

"Oh my God, no, not that exquisite face. She's so beautiful."

"She still is. Brandon, this is serious. She doesn't want anyone to know, and she doesn't want press or social media or people intruding on her. She's traveling a hard road, and she needs our support. You're the only person who knows now, other than myself and my staff. I don't want her to know that you found out. She'd be very upset."

"Of course," Brandon said, looking devastated. "Can she walk?"

"Yes." Edward knew he had to tell him something—the poor man looked heartbroken. She was so gentle and endearing that

The Portrait

people loved her, and she had obviously won Brandon Yates's heart during his sittings for the portrait. Her sincerity and innocence and pure goodness cast a spell on everyone who knew her. "She's having some problems with her vision." Brandon looked shocked again.

"Oh God, no. Can she paint?"

Edward hesitated. "Not yet, but I'm sure she will again. Now you know why it's important you not say anything."

"I give you my solemn word of honor," Brandon said, with tears in his eyes that spilled onto his cheeks, which touched Edward. He had cried over it too. Even Tom Kingsley, who was tough as nails, had cried when he heard the news of the accident. Devon didn't deserve this after the hardships she had endured earlier. "Can I see her?" Brandon asked.

"I don't think she'd want you to yet. It's still early days. It happened literally right after she finished your portrait, the same day. It's been about five weeks. This could resolve quickly, or be a long haul. We don't know."

"A car accident?"

"Chemicals. Cleaning her brushes."

"What can I do?" Brandon wanted to help.

"Send her good thoughts, and texts, not letting on that you know. I'll keep you posted, but it looks like progress could be slow."

"I wish I could see her."

It occurred to Edward then that Brandon's exuberance might cheer her up. He seemed to genuinely love her as a friend.

"Let's hope that when you do, we can celebrate her full recovery." Brandon nodded, looking thoughtful and badly shaken.

"It couldn't . . . she won't be . . . she isn't . . . ?" He couldn't say the word.

"I am hoping for a full recovery. Anything is possible. And a miracle right about now would be most welcome."

"I'm going to start praying. I'll go on a fast for her. That can be very powerful," Brandon said, and Edward tried not to look amused. Brandon was very Hollywood. "And meditation. I meditate every day."

"Whatever works," Edward said. And he was suddenly tempted to let him see her.

"What happened to the boyfriend? Did he come back?" Brandon asked him, and Edward looked surprised.

"Boyfriend? Is there a boyfriend? I didn't know." He was astonished to hear it. There was no sign of a man in Devon's life.

"Not really. For about five minutes. They met last summer and she liked him. He broke it off with her immediately, and she was upset. He came back and then disappeared again." Brandon filled him in.

"More fool he. She's the nicest woman I know. And she doesn't need a guy like that," Edward said with a disapproving look.

"That's what I told her. I guess he never came back. He ditched her and never contacted her again while she did my portrait. I caught her crying a few times, so she told me."

"Bastard," Edward growled, protective of her. "No, there's no one around, just the nurses and me. She has no visitors." Edward knew how private and discreet she was, and how professional, so she must have been very upset if she told Brandon about it.

"Even my dog loves her," Brandon volunteered. "Maybe I'll send

The Portrait

her a video of me and Thornton, just to say we miss her and love her, without letting on that I know anything."

"She might like that." Even if she couldn't see it, she could hear it, and Edward could see that Brandon meant well—even if he was a bit of Hollywood flash, he seemed deeply sincere about Devon. Brandon hugged him before he left, and said he'd be in touch, and Edward sat musing about the mysterious boyfriend who had "ditched her," and the fact that Devon had resisted Brandon Yates's charms. Few women did. She was an honorable woman and the guy who had dumped her was clearly a jerk. And he certainly wasn't around. Edward wondered if he knew. Probably not, if he had cut off communication with her.

Edward went back to work then, hoping that Brandon wouldn't talk. He thought he could trust him not to, out of concern for Devon. If his meditation brought on a miracle, so much the better.

When he went home, Brandon had an idea, and got to work on his computer to do some research. Maybe there was something he could do for his beloved friend after all.

February wasn't easy for Devon. The treatments were painful and weren't doing anything. There was no progress at all. She could see light and dark and nothing more distinct than that. The doctors weren't ready to give up and send her home or to rehab. The doctor at Mass General said that at least another month of treatments every two hours should be the protocol before reassessing her situation and the prognosis. And he agreed that surgery wouldn't help. But it was hard to keep believing with no results. Edward was worried to find her so very down when he visited. He told her how much Brandon loved his portrait and she referred to it several times as "my last portrait" with a finality that upset him deeply.

On Valentine's Day, one of the nurses said that they were doing a party for the children in pediatrics, and Devon had an idea. She asked her private duty nurse to get her a big roll of white paper and red markers. She sent her out to get it, and spoke to one of the floor nurses.

"I'd like to do a sign for the children. I sent my nurse out for a roll of white paper, and some markers. If someone can guide my hand so I place it correctly on the paper, I can do red hearts, and my nurse can color them. I can do the hearts, I just need her to help me space them correctly." The head nurse on her floor thought it would be good for her. Devon had been despondent lately, and the children would love the sign. They already had balloons for the children, donated by one of the mothers, and one of the nurses had brought cupcakes from home.

When her day nurse came back with the paper and markers, Devon helped her roll it out on the floor, and got down on her hands and knees and told the nurse to tell her how far to space them. She drew the hearts with mechanical precision and covered a long roll of the paper with them in an hour. The private duty nurse followed along behind her filling the hearts in with the red marker. The result was a very professional-looking long sign like a banner. They could even cut it to make it into shorter ones.

The Portrait

Devon and her Irish nurse had spent an hour crawling around on the floor to make the sign, and when they were finished, they took it out to the nurses' desk. It was beautiful, and the nurses were excited. Two of them took it to Pediatrics to tape it up. It made Devon happy to do it, and everyone loved it.

While Devon was making the Valentine's Day sign for Pediatrics, Brandon Yates showed up at the gallery and asked to see Edward. He had been working on an idea for the two weeks since he'd seen him.

"I need your help. Maybe it's a crazy idea and she'll hate it, but I had to do something." What Brandon had done was as crazy and kind as he was, had taken a great deal of time, and was expensive. Edward listened and doubted they'd get away with it, but Brandon was so passionate about it, Edward didn't have the heart to turn him down. It meant that Devon would know that Brandon knew of her accident, which she might forgive him for. She desperately needed cheering up after nearly two months in a hospital. The hospital was going to be the stumbling block, but Edward was willing to help. There was something endearing and innocent about Brandon that reminded him of Devon. And Edward was used to crazy artists, although most of theirs were staid, and very serious. But there were a few who were flamboyant and zany. And Edward always liked them. Tom Kingsley was less amused by the crazy ones.

"So what do we do?" Brandon asked him.

"Leave it to me. I'll make some calls. I made a big donation last month, and Devon just made one. That should help. I'm going to call the head of the hospital board and beg. Begging usually works.

Groveling is a good skill to have too. I'm willing to try both. If they say yes, I'll meet you at the hospital later today. In theory I don't like the implication that her current problem is forever, but since you say it's versatile, then I'm all for it as a spirit booster."

"It's Valentine's Day," Brandon reminded him.

"Exactly. I'll remind the head of the board of that between groveling and begging."

"I hope it works," Brandon said earnestly, praying for victory. And Edward was an excellent partner in crime, better than he had expected.

Brandon waited all day for Edward's call and was losing hope when Edward called him at four-thirty and gave a whoop of victory. "We won! We're in. They said to come after visiting hours end. That's eight o'clock on her floor, when they give the patients their meds for the night, and all the conditions you listed for me have to hold. If there is any slippage, we're out, but they won't throw Devon out. So it's worth a shot." Brandon had made all the arrangements and covered all the bases. He had promised Edward it would work, and if not he would keep the gift he had planned for Devon until she got home. He was so excited he could hardly stand it.

"I'll meet you at the side entrance at quarter to eight. The head of the board emailed me a letter I'll carry with me, guaranteeing us safe passage."

"Terrific! We'll be there," Brandon said. It was better than an espionage mission in a movie, and he thought Devon would love it.

* * *

The Portrait

At a quarter to eight that night, they met with military precision at the side door to the hospital, and were ready to go. Brandon had a bag of supplies with him, with more to be delivered the next day, and Edward looked at his companion and was shocked.

"Oh my God, it's a horse, not a dog."

"My dog is much bigger," Brandon assured him. "Wendy was the runt of her litter." She was a sleek, elegant, dark chocolate brown and perfectly behaved bullmastiff who sat at attention and offered Edward a polite paw. "Right paw is thank you," Brandon explained. "Left is hello." She was holding out her left, and she was wearing a guide dog harness, and was a licensed service dog. She was a bullmastiff like Thornton, only much smaller. She was still a very large dog, but not compared to him. Brandon had scoured the country for her and had found her in Kentucky. She was an experienced guide dog whose previous owner had had cornea transplants and left for college, so she had been retired and returned to the breeder. She was four years old and responded to voice commands. The harness was more to identify her as a service dog than to control her. Edward had a letter with him from the head of the hospital board allowing them to enter with a service dog.

Edward and Brandon walked into the hospital nonchalantly, and a security guard glanced at the dog, saw the harness, and nodded them through. The same happened at the metal detector, and people in the elevator smiled at them, as they rode up to Devon's floor.

They walked past the nurses' desk with an air of authority, and the nurses were all busy measuring out meds and paid no attention. They walked to the Governor's Suite, opened the door, and slipped through, and Edward spoke immediately so Devon would know he was there. But she always knew anyway. She said she could recognize the faint smell of the cologne he wore, and his soap.

"Happy Valentine's Day!" Edward said as he walked in. The private duty nurse opened her eyes wide in surprise and he put a finger to his lips, and she nodded. "I brought a friend to visit you," he said, and she frowned. She didn't want visitors, but she didn't want to be rude, and then she cocked her head to one side as though sensing something. Brandon unhooked Wendy's leash then, and she went straight to Devon, sitting in a chair, and nuzzled her hand. Devon had been listening to a podcast about Leonardo da Vinci on her iPad. She had found a series of them, about the greatest artists in history.

Devon looked confused for a minute, and then she felt the sleek coat, and the cold nose, and Wendy gave her the hello paw, and Devon laughed and looked in Edward's direction as Brandon's eyes filled with tears. Devon was just as beautiful as before but he could tell that she couldn't see her visitors.

"Oh my God, Edward, it's a dog, how did you get it in here?"

"I got special permission. And I groveled to get it," he said, and she laughed. "Her name is Wendy, and she's a gift, you can keep her if you like." Wendy had put her paws on Devon's knees and was licking her face.

She was grinning. "She's big." And then she felt Wendy's face carefully, and said in a tone of surprise, "I think she's the same kind as Brandon's dog Thornton, only she's smaller." And then she looked around, straight in Brandon's direction and sniffed the air. She had developed all of her other faculties in the seven weeks

The Portrait

she'd been blind. "Brandon, are you here too? I can smell your cologne—Givenchy. Where are you?" She looked happy when she said it.

"I'm here, baby," he said gently. "I came with Wendy."

"She's a guide dog, right?" Devon felt the harness and looked in his direction as he approached, even though she couldn't see him. She could feel him in the room. "But what if I don't need her later, if... you know?"

"She does regular gigs too, she's very versatile. Cooks, does dishes, tap dances, sings," he said, as the nurse wiped tears off her cheeks. It was such a sweet scene. Devon wrapped her arms around Wendy's neck and held her, and the dog kissed her again.

"Can I keep her here?" she asked the room in general.

"You can, as long as you keep her in your room," Edward said. "She can't wander the halls."

"She has a dog walker who'll come three times a day, a trainer who'll work with you and her, voice coach, drama coach, hairdresser, colorist, you know, the usual," Brandon said, and she laughed and held her arms out to him, and he walked toward her and gave her a hug. She seemed so fragile he was afraid to hurt her.

"My arms aren't broken, I'm fine." But she looked pale and frail to him, and she'd lost weight. Her bright red hair was in a braid and there were no bandages on her eyes—she had taken them off to air her eyes for a while. Wendy was staying close to her, and already knew who she belonged to, and then she trotted across the room to check out the bed, stood up on it and got down, as Devon stared in her direction. She kept staring and didn't talk, and then she whispered, "I can see her... Oh my God... I can see her . . . not her face, her shape." Wendy was standing on the bed again, in profile. Devon stood up so she could see her better and then she looked in Brandon's direction. "I can see your shape too. You have something on your head . . . a baseball cap . . . and I can see Edward . . . I can't see your faces, but I see your outlines," she said in a stunned voice. It was the first progress she had made in weeks, and it was major. Both men were crying and hugged each other, and the nurse was crying and Devon was too, as Wendy watched them, got off the bed and came to stand next to Devon. "I can see shapes," she said again. "I see my bed." She looked around the room at the outlines she could make out. It was an incredible Valentine's Day gift, as was Wendy. After they recovered from the shock of the quantum leap she had just taken, Brandon showed her and the nurse Wendy's food, her treats, a rolled-up soft bed in the bag, and some toys.

"I'll send you more stuff tomorrow." And Edward said they should leave soon before they got thrown out. He left Wendy's permission letter with the nurse. Both men hugged Devon, and were shaken when they left, as Devon sat on her bed with the dog, stroking her.

"It's a miracle," Edward said to Brandon as they walked down the hall, and he wiped tears off his cheeks again.

"I told you, meditation and fasting, it never fails," Brandon said, as Edward realized what had just happened. She was starting to see again. It was coming back.

"I'm starting to fast tomorrow," Edward said, and put an arm around Brandon's shoulders. Both men were smiling broadly. Mission accomplished. With a Valentine's Day miracle thrown in.

Chapter 14

For the next six weeks, Devon's progress was erratic. It didn't happen in a straight line. But more and more of her vision came back, slowly but steadily. At first she only saw shapes, and then the blur inside the shapes came clearer. She saw faces, and sometimes details. Seeing colors clearly took longer. It was exciting every day to discover what she could see that day. Her depth perception wasn't good at first, which made her dizzy and she stumbled, and then that went away too. And Wendy was at her side every moment. Some of the nurses didn't like it, but they couldn't object because she was a legal service dog. And Devon loved her. She looked like a much smaller version of Thornton, and she wanted to paint her. She was a noble-looking dog and adored Devon.

By the end of March, Devon could see again. It had taken three months. Brandon continued to visit her until he had to leave to start filming a movie in California, and Wendy was the greatest gift of her life.

Edward was there every day. He hadn't prayed in years but he had prayed for her.

She had numerous consultations with the doctors, and a long Zoom meeting with the manufacturers of the solution that had blinded her. They were taking out two of the lethal ingredients before putting it back on the market. And the doctor at Mass General documented her entire case. None of them were exactly sure what part of her many treatments had brought her vision back, and they warned her not to overdo it.

"Can I paint now?" she asked Dr. Allen, who was almost as pleased as she was that she could see again.

"Three hours a day, tops," was his answer. "If you have no problem between now and June, you can go back to work full-time in the summer." She and Edward had reorganized her commission schedule. She was going to do light work until the end of June, go to the Hamptons as she always did in July and August, and take it easy. And she would start back to her real work on the first of September, or after Labor Day. Her waiting list was long now with the people who had waited for her. They thought it was worth it.

Edward knew it would be hard for her to limit herself to three hours a day, but she had to. She didn't want to go blind again, and she had to protect her eyes from the sun and bright lights.

Devon was grateful every day when she woke up that she could see.

She left the hospital exactly three months to the day after she'd arrived, screaming and panicked and blind. Wendy trotted along beside her, and was fascinated by her new home. Devon's private duty nurses had promised to visit her. They had become friends in the three months they took care of her, and had been her eyes when she had none. It was the most frightening experience of her life, and she would never take her sight for granted again. Every color, every object she could see, every face was a gift, as she walked around her home in awe. And Edward had been the father she never had. He had come to see her almost every day, and called her daily when she got home. They had been through an incredible experience together. Regaining her sight had restored Edward's faith in the goodness of life, and that good things did happen.

Devon put away her things from the hospital, and tidied up. Her easel was empty, and the paint on it was dry. Her brushes still lay helter-skelter where she had left them the night of the accident. She would wear a shield now when she cleaned them, so not a speck of chemicals could get in her eyes.

She was going through the drawers in her studio, just seeing what was there, when she came across a manila envelope and opened it. They were the photographs of Charlie on his boat. She stood looking at them for a long time. He looked so happy, and they had been so happy. He was part of history now, and it seemed like a long time ago. She still thought about him, and missed him at times, but he was as far away now as the people she had loved and lost. She knew she would never see him again and it was okay. She didn't expect to, as if Charlie were someone who had died, except that he was in the world somewhere and she wished him well. She had let him go. She had been through so much since then, it made a broken romance seem so much less important. Her heart didn't ache now when she thought of him.

She spread the photographs out on her work table. There were a lot of them, and she had some favorites. And then she had an idea. She had wondered what she would paint for three hours a day. She had canceled Charlie's portrait, which was what he had wanted from her in the first place.

It didn't hurt, looking at his photographs now. It felt bittersweet.

Devon dug through her blank canvases to see if she had one the right size. At first she thought horizontal, and then she thought a tall vertical, a big canvas, with the sails fluttering above him as he stood on deck at the helm, in front of the mast. She found a very big vertical canvas in her storeroom. She usually used them for very formal portraits. Older men liked them, or women in ball gowns. But it seemed just right for the photographs she had of Charlie. It would take forever to paint a big canvas like that in only three hours a day. But she had no commissions until September, and if she felt like it, she could take it to the Hamptons and finish it there. It was an exciting project and she couldn't wait to paint again. It seemed funny that she was going to start with a portrait of Charlie. But why not? She could do whatever she wanted for the next five months before she went back to her real work, and as her eyes continued to rest and heal.

She got up early the next morning and set the canvas on her easel. She had cleaned her brushes with old-fashioned turpentine the night before. It was a familiar smell, and reminded her of the Beaux-Arts school in Paris. And with a cup of coffee beside her, she began sketching and laying down the underlay. She hadn't decided on the background yet. Maybe just the ocean with some whitecaps in a light wind in the distance. She could almost feel the

The Portrait

sea breeze on her face from that day seven months ago. And as she stood smelling the paints and the turpentine, standing at her easel, mixing the tones for the underlayer, and glancing at the photographs, it felt so good to be back. And Wendy lay at her feet while she worked. She never left Devon's side.

Charlie had been busy in March too. He had moved out of the big house he and Faye had sold, sent things to storage, sold others, sent Faye what she wanted in Aspen, and put some things in storage for her too, for the condo she was going to buy, her new home away from Aspen. Working remotely suited her and she liked it. She was tired of going to an office.

He had moved into his new smaller house, which he would share some of the time with Liam. It was immaculately clean, everything looked brand-new, and the things he had brought with him fit perfectly in the new house. It felt meant to be.

He had decided to accept the offer from Texas and sell his business. Faye was right. It was time. He wanted to make a clean sweep and start fresh. It took until May to finish the negotiations and sign the deal. He felt like a free man now that he no longer had a billion-dollar company on his shoulders. The new owners were going to take it public. Charlie wanted to start a new company that he could grow and watch thrive. That was the exciting part for him. He was in love with startups, not the grand dames of business, like banks. He liked mapping it out and designing it, the way Liam was doing with his gardens. Liam had almost finished the course in Normandy and was making noises about staying in

France. He hadn't been back to see the new house yet, but he promised to come that summer. But Charlie didn't think Liam had France out of his system yet, and he was still dating the same girl. Charlie hoped he wouldn't marry her or get her pregnant. At twenty-three, Liam was way too young to make a lifetime commitment, or even a long-term one. Charlie had learned that lesson the hard way.

His divorce was going to be final at the end of June, and when it was, he would be totally unfettered. He'd be a man without a wife, without a business, without a big house to tie him down, and only a smaller one, although it was very luxurious. He could go wherever he wanted, and do as he pleased. It was what he had wanted, and he was happy with his recent decisions, but there was a slightly hollow feel, with no one to share any of it with. Devon still crossed his mind, and he realized he had made terrible mistakes with her, letting her get away, and he knew he had hurt her badly, and hadn't forgiven himself for it. He had learned his lessons at her expense, which was so wrong. The past few months had freed him—the divorce, the big house, the business. He should have done all of it a long time ago, but he wasn't ready. He hadn't been ready for Devon either. She had actually lost more and been in better shape. He blamed himself for being cowardly, for not being brave enough to move forward with her, and he knew he'd always regret it.

He was looking forward to the summer in the Hamptons. He had nothing to rush home to. He could stay for as long as he wanted. He had a stack of business plans to read, of young companies he might want to invest in, or startups that might excite him.

The Portrait

He loved the idea of starting something new in business. He still had a passion for it.

On the spur of the moment, Charlie decided to visit Liam in France in June, and see him get his diploma for the classes and projects he had done there for a year. Liam had given up the idea of graduate school at Yale. He was looking for a job with an established landscape architecture firm, in France, England, or California, whoever offered him the best opportunity. At twenty-three he could go wherever he wanted, and intended to. He was still learning his craft, and he had talent with anything that involved earth and gardens and land. He was a man of the earth, unlike his father.

Charlie met his girlfriend, Sabine, and liked her. She was a nice young woman, with a green thumb. Her dream was to own a high-end florist shop one day and do beautiful decor for fashion shows or big parties or balls. She came from a family of doctors who wanted her to go to medical school. Her mother was a gynecologist, her father a cardiologist, her brother an orthopedic surgeon, and Sabine couldn't imagine anything worse than blood and gore and carving up bodies all day long. She wanted to work with beauty and flowers. And Liam said she had talent. She was the same age as he was. They had a lifetime ahead of them to make good and bad decisions, and Charlie was sure they'd make many of both, just as he had. He tried to stay open-minded about it, particularly since Faye always thought she knew best what Liam should be doing, and they argued constantly about it. Charlie had no desire to run his son's life and knew better. It was a lesson Faye hadn't learned yet, and maybe never would, like his father. He realized now that he had married a woman who was very much like his father.

It was a new discipline for Devon, learning to paint only three hours a day when she was sailing along and could have gone on for ten or twelve hours longer. She had the stamina to paint long hours, but she had to protect her eyes now until they were stronger. They felt fine, but she had promised to follow the doctor's orders, and knowing her work mode, Edward reminded her of it often when he called her. He didn't know what she was working on and she didn't tell him, but he could guess that she had gone straight to her easel and paints when she got home. Once Devon got going on a painting she couldn't stop herself, but she had to now. She set an alarm every day so she would know when her three hours were up and she had to stop.

Despite the shortened work hours, she finished the painting of Charlie in late June, and she loved it. Because she had taken the photographs of him during a magical time for them, doing what he loved most on his little sailboat, with the woman he loved, the painting exuded pure joy, and the love of the sea, and his eyes had been full of love as he looked straight at her when she took the photographs of him. It was a beautiful portrait, and she loved looking at it. She could feel the wind fill the sails of the little sailboat, and almost smell the sea. And he looked so real, he looked like he was about to speak.

She knew where the portrait belonged, and she was going to send it to him. His was the only commission she had canceled, not postponed, because he wanted no contact with her, and probably still didn't, and she was fine with it now. But she wanted him to have the painting as a gift.

She called the gallery when the painting was dry, and asked them if they would ship a painting to California for her.

"Of course," Edward's secretary told her. Devon was sending it to Charlie's office at the bank, which was the only address she had for him, and it had to be crated to get there safely.

She rented a van to get it to the gallery and dropped it off. Wendy came everywhere with her and was enjoying her new life. Devon kept her guide dog harness on her to show that she was a service dog in case anyone stopped them, which they rarely did.

She was sad to see the last of the painting, but she wanted Charlie to have it. She had put her heart and soul into it. She asked Edward's secretary to include a formal note with it. "A gift from the artist." And she scribbled on the note when she dropped off the painting. "I owed you one for the cancellation. D." She dropped the van off then, and she and Wendy walked home. With a dog that size at her side, with or without the harness, Devon was safe anywhere. She sent Brandon photos of her from time to time. He was having fun on the movie, and the tabloids claimed he was having a white-hot affair with the star, who was twenty-five years younger than he was. She had broken up with her boyfriend, and she and Brandon were about to get engaged. Devon smiled when she saw it, and was happy Brandon was having fun. She was grateful to him for Wendy every day. She and Wendy loved each other.

* * *

She left for East Hampton the following week, driven by a car service with a van big enough for Wendy, who sat on the seat next to Devon and looked out the window. Devon was happy to be back. She hadn't come all winter because of the accident. Her cleaning service had cleaned the barn thoroughly before she arrived, and Wendy loved exploring the garden, barking at deer in the distance, and running down the beach with Devon. Devon felt free and alive to be in the sun and the ocean again. She had to wear goggles when she swam and dark glasses in the sun, but it was a small price to pay for having her sight back. The doctors had released her at the end of June, and she could paint now for as long as she wanted. Her life was back to normal after six brutally rugged months.

Edward saw the portrait of Charlie before they shipped it out, and he wondered who Charles Taylor was in San Francisco. It rang a bell and Edward looked it up in their records. He was the only commission Devon had canceled, and they had refunded his money. And now she was sending him a gift. She had the right to do that, and Edward wondered who he was. He suddenly remembered what Brandon had told him about the "jerk" who had shut her out and upset her. Edward was curious about him, but he didn't want to ask. The painting was beautiful and Edward hoped Charlie deserved it as a gift. They sent it to California priority two days later, to a bank, and Edward noted Charlie's title, Chairman of the Board.

Devon was in the Hamptons by the time the painting arrived in San Francisco. And Charlie was preparing to leave for the Hamptons himself.

The Portrait

One of the assistants called to tell him a crate had arrived for him at the bank. A very large wooden crate.

"I didn't buy anything," he said, puzzled.

"It looks like it could be a painting," she said.

"Take a look at the waybill, and see who it's from. It sounds like a mistake."

She was back a minute later. "Kingsley and Stone, on Madison Avenue in New York. Should I send it back?" she asked efficiently. Charlie's heart skipped a beat when he heard who had sent it.

"No. I'll come take a look at it tomorrow. I have to come into the city." He was curious to see what they had sent him. Maybe they were trying to sell him a painting and had sent it on approval for him to see.

He thought about it that night, and about Devon, drove to the city the next morning, and went straight to the bank.

He got one of the maintenance men to lend him the tools to open the wooden crate. He found Devon's note before he saw the painting, and he couldn't imagine what she had sent him as a gift. He knew he didn't deserve a gift from her, or anything else. It was a moment in his life he wasn't proud of and had handled badly, at her expense. He knew he would remember their brief time together forever.

The painting was professionally wrapped, and Charlie peeled away the layers of paper and protection and wrestled it out of the crate. It stood as tall as he was, and he had to turn it on its side to get it out, and when he leaned it up against his desk and saw it, it took his breath away. It was painted in her extraordinary style of reality mixed with magic, with the wind and the sails and the sea and the joy on his face, and the love in his eyes that he had extinguished so quickly. But Devon had immortalized it, and it was all there in the moment. A fleeting moment in their life.

Charlie had one of the assistants at the bank hire a van to take it to his home and he stood staring at it when it got there. It was an exquisitely beautiful painting, and an enormous gift. He didn't want to call her or write to her, and he thought about stopping to see her in New York on his way to the Hamptons. He owed her an apology as well as his thanks, face-to-face, if she would see him. He was afraid she wouldn't.

He was flying east the next day, and he would drive in from Teterboro. He knew she didn't go to the Hamptons until the end of June, and thought she might still be in the city.

Charlie thought about Devon all the way the next day on the flight. They had shared so little, but it had been so perfect. He remembered the Thanksgiving he had spent with her and the last time he'd seen her when he kissed her goodbye. Adam had been right. He was a coward.

Once he got to Teterboro, it seemed a long way to go just to thank her, and she probably wouldn't see him. But he knew it was the right thing to do. He had to at least try. Sending him the painting was an enormously generous gesture—he could at least make a small one. He had the car that was waiting to take him to East Hampton drive him into the city. It was a long detour in summer traffic, but he felt compelled to see her and thank her in person.

Memories of her filled his mind and his heart as they drove down her street. He remembered how familiar it had all felt when

The Portrait

he was there, a warm eclectic neighborhood filled with real people. Devon was real, like no one else he had ever known.

The car stopped at her address and he got out and looked up at her building. He felt slightly sick remembering what he had done and how cruel he had been, and how hurt she must have been by it. There was no way he could make up for it now. All he could do was say thank you for the painting, tell her he was sorry, and wish her well.

There was a handyman painting the flowerboxes in front of the house. He watched Charlie climb the stairs and ring the bell. No one answered and the man in painter's overalls called up to him. "She's not here, she's gone." Charlie wasn't sure what to say. He had nothing to deliver except an apology and his thanks. "For the summer," the handyman added. "You got a package to leave?" Charlie shook his head. He felt foolish standing there.

"I'm just a friend, stopping by to see how she is," he said. A friend who obviously didn't know where she was.

"Oh, she's okay now. She got out of the hospital a couple of months ago." Charlie's blood ran cold when he said it.

"The hospital? I didn't know. I live in California." He wanted to know what the man would say now.

"Yeah, she had a bad accident. Real bad, but she's good now. She was in the hospital for months. She was blind but now she's good again," the handyman said, filling Charlie in on the news. Charlie was horrified by what he'd said.

"I'm glad she's okay," Charlie kept up the conversation. "Is she in the Hamptons?"

"I don't know. She don't tell me. I think so. She left early for the beach this year. She's not working yet."

"Well, thanks very much," Charlie said, and he waved and got back in his car as the man went on painting. Charlie was stunned. She had had an accident and was in the hospital and had gone blind. She obviously wasn't blind now, if she had done the painting. Or maybe she'd done it before. He felt even worse now for his silence. And she had sent him the painting anyway.

He told the driver he was ready to head for East Hampton, and was prepared for a long drive in summer traffic. It gave him plenty of time to mull over what the handyman had said. He didn't see how he could face her now. He had told her he loved her and abandoned her cruelly. He didn't know how she could forgive him for it, and even less how he could forgive himself. All he knew was that he had to see her one more time, to tell her he was sorry. The painting was the icing on the cake, and yet one more sign of what a kind, gracious person she was, and he had never deserved her.

Chapter 15

Charlie greeted the couple who took care of the house, and set his bags down in his bedroom. He took a walk on the beach at sunset, and it felt good to be back. The smell of the sea air, the sand under his feet, the breeze off the ocean. It felt wholesome and sane. His life had been out of control for a long time and now it was manageable. He wasn't afraid anymore. Everything had changed, and he had grown and changed with it. Everything he had been afraid of had happened, and it wasn't so bad. The worst part was losing Devon, running away from her, being too afraid to be with her and stand beside her. And something terrible had happened to her, and he hadn't been there. He could only imagine what going blind and fearing never being able to paint again would have been like for her. She must have been terrified, and she hadn't called him, because he had abandoned her. He had no idea what to say to her now. There were no words to tell her how sorry he was. And she probably didn't care. Why would she? But she had cared enough to send him the painting and he wanted to thank her for it. At least he could do that. Real courage was standing in front of someone you love, knowing you had hurt them, and being able to face them. He owed her at least that.

He looked far down the beach and saw a woman running with an enormous dog. She was throwing a ball for it, and it kept running away from her and back again. She chased the dog into the surf. The dog was barking and leaping and she was laughing. As they came closer, Charlie saw that it was Devon, her hair loose in the wind. She looked happy and free. He smiled, watching them as they approached. She was so intent on the dog, she didn't see him. For a moment, he wanted to hide, or run away, but he couldn't do that anymore, and didn't really want to. He had to face her, at least once, and then she never had to see him again. She had lived the last seven months without him, and she looked happy.

As she slowed to a walk, she saw him, and looked startled. The dog was still running and playing. Devon looked serious as Charlie walked toward her. Destiny had brought them together again, but he would have gone to see her anyway. He could never stay away from her, and then he'd run away. He wasn't running anymore. There were no demons left. She took off her dark glasses as he approached, and he could see her green eyes shining in the sun. He wished he had a portrait of her to remember her by, just like this, on the beach, with her wild red hair flying in the wind.

"I owe you an apology and a thank-you," he said when he was standing in front of her.

"Not really. I'm fine." She smiled at him then. "The painting is good though, isn't it? I had fun doing it. It was so perfectly you, on

The Portrait

your sailboat." And she was so perfectly her, standing in front of him. It made his heart ache to look at her, she was so beautiful and so brave. She could hide in her art. He had nowhere to hide. He felt naked, and ashamed of how he had treated her. "I'm sorry I canceled your portrait. I had an accident. I was out of commission for a few months. Your painting is the first one I worked on when I got back. I wanted you to have it."

"I don't deserve it, after my disappearing act."

"You missed some bad months," she said simply. "I'm fine now. And grateful. How are you?"

He smiled at the question. "It's been interesting. I sold my business, and my house. I bought a smaller house, and I'm looking for a new business to start. And my divorce will be final on Friday. I can't take credit for it. It was Faye's idea. Best idea she's ever had, and we're friends."

"You've been busy." Devon smiled at him as the dog ran between them, playing, and almost knocked them down. "I went blind and got my sight back. That's all I did. Wendy brought me luck. She's a guide dog, and I started to get my sight back the day I got her."

"I'm sorry I wasn't there." She could see he meant it.

"Me too. But I survived. You survived. We're survivors. I grew from it. It was terrifying being blind. But most of the time the things we fear most don't happen, and when they do, we get through them somehow." Devon had been to the worst and back, and now she was walking on the beach and playing with her dog, and Charlie was standing there talking to her. The man she had lost. And now here he was. She kept a little distance from him, afraid to get too close. She didn't want to get hurt again. He was history for her.

"I'm sorry I was such a coward," he said.

"You weren't a coward, you were human. I was scared too. I'm not anymore. The old ghosts are at peace and I can see again. It's enough." As she looked at him she realized she had forgiven him months ago for hurting her. He might hurt her again, if she let him, or he might not. Living meant taking risks, getting hurt, loving, being happy, being sad, taking a chance on life.

"Can I ask you to the house for a glass of wine?" he asked her. She hesitated, and smiled.

"Sure." He took her hand and they ran down the beach, laughing, with the dog following them into the future.

About the Author

DANIELLE STEEL has been hailed as one of the world's bestselling authors, with a billion copies of her novels sold. Her many international bestsellers include *For Richer For Poorer, A Mother's Love, A Mind of Her Own, Far From Home, Never Say Never, Trial by Fire, Triangle, Joy,* and other highly acclaimed novels. She is also the author of *His Bright Light,* the story of her son Nick Traina's life and death; *A Gift of Hope,* a memoir of her work with the homeless; *Expect a Miracle,* a book of her favorite quotations for inspiration and comfort; *Pure Joy,* about the dogs she and her family have loved; and the children's books *Pretty Minnie in Paris* and *Pretty Minnie in Hollywood.*

daniellesteel.com
Facebook.com/DanielleSteelOfficial
Instagram: @officialdaniellesteel

About the Type

This book was set in Charter, a typeface designed in 1987 by Matthew Carter (b. 1937) for Bitstream, Inc., a digital typefoundry that he cofounded in 1981. One of the most influential typographers of our time, Carter designed this versatile font to feature a compact width, squared serifs, and open letterforms. These features give the typeface a fresh, highly legible, and unencumbered appearance.